The Greek Rule

By
Aleka Nakis

Electronic release: July 2012

To my friend, Kate.

Thanks for pushing me into believing it was possible.

The endless morning re-reads were the highlight of my days.

Here is your book!

The Greek Rule's Greek-English Guide

Mou: is the possessive Greek term of my
Agape mou: my love
Antra mou: my man/ my husband
Baba: dad
Cardia mou: my heart
Despinis: Miss
Dropi: shame
Gia mas: cheers
Gineka mou: my woman/ my wife
Kalimera: good morning
Alinihta: good night/evening
Kalithea: good view
Kori mou: my daughter
Koukla mou: my doll
Koumbaroi: sponsors at a wedding or christening
Komboloi: beads strung together on a chain and traditionally used by men
Kyria: Mrs.
Mama: mom
Paidi mou: my child
Pame: let us go
Panda: forever
Pethera: mother-in-law
Theo: uncle
Thea: aunt
Yiayia: grandmother
And a term you can use for almost anything in Greek:
Gia! : Hello, goodbye, to your health, bless you, cheers!

Chapter One

Two months to learn from the best hotelier in the world, then, if everything went as planned, Athena Lakis wouldn't be working for someone else. She did enjoy her job. She loved it. But Athena had always dreamed of running her own empire.

Sitting opposite the man who'd agreed to make it all possible her boss, Lucas Giardetti, she relayed the last minute details of the Naples Children Charity Ball. It was Athena's last big project under her current position. She'd worked hard to make the event a huge success for Giardetti Worldwide Hospitality. Honestly, it was the least she could do in appreciation for the opportunity they had given her. The charity ball was the cherry on the whipped cream, and she wanted everything to go just right.

The florist had delivered the proper shade of pink freesias, even if it had taken him three tries. The 1969 Vintage Dom chilled at the perfect temperature, even if upon delivery it had been two degrees too warm. They weren't spending that kind of money to drink warm champagne. And the maitre d'hotel had reassigned the waiter who didn't own an iron to a different function. She didn't want the young man to lose his job. She simply didn't want him serving guests while wearing wrinkled attire.

No, this night was too important for anything to be off by a single degree. The sponsors of the Naples Children Charity appreciated the worthiness of the cause, but they also expected pampering for their great generosity.

Suddenly distracted, she froze when the most striking man she'd ever see entered her peripheral vision. Her abdomen tightened, her heart raced, and she had to work very hard to her keep breathing steady as he walked across the hotel lounge, maneuvering around the antique tables in her direction. She didn't need the disturbance of this Adonis male three hours before the fundraising ball began.

Making a conscious effort not to look beyond the dossier she reviewed with Luca, she attempted to continue with her final report. "The guests will arrive from the south entrance between eight and nine. Cocktails will begin with—"

"Hello, my friend." Luca rose to greet the man commanding Athena's attention. Standing a handsome six-foot-two, Luca was not a small man, but the obvious confidence and physical appearance of the tall, broad stranger with the dark eyes and bright smile dwarfed her employer. "I am so glad you could make it to Naples for the ball. What is it? At least three months since we sat together for anything other than business. We have some catching up to do."

"My thoughts exactly," drawled the sexy stranger in an accent that was more than a little familiar to her. He did not wait for an introduction. Rather he took Athena's hand and gently raised it to his lips. His warm breath caressed her skin, sending a parade of tingles through her body. "I can see why you choose to work such long hours."

There was playful recognition in his eyes. He must know her, or know of her. She was curiously aware of the familiarity in his tone, but she couldn't place him. Who was this man who sucked every bit of air from the lounge?

She mentally searched the evening's guest list, but the shape of his eyes and the set of his jaw did it. Suddenly, she knew who he was.

Drop dead gorgeous competition!

Not only was he bidding against her dream, he was soon to be related to her best friend.

Dumbfounded, she stared at her best friend's future brother-in-law and the head of Strintzaris Enterprises. She'd had no idea her boss kept the competition as a close friend.

Shifting in her seat, she waited for him to say something about the property they were both fighting for in Crete. DDGC sat atop the Strintzaris mega-empire, while she hid within the coattails of Luca Giardetti's name.

Luca smiled and made the introduction. "Alexandros Strintzaris, this is Athena Lakis. Miss Lakis chairs the consulting committee responsible for the symposium."

"I'm very pleased to finally meet you, Athena."

"Likewise." Trying unsuccessfully to retrieve her burning hand, she broadened her smile.

"Athena is a great force within Giardetti. She doesn't climb the rungs on the corporate ladder, she jumps over them."

"Ah, but what a pleasure it would be to lure her to Strintzaris Enterprises. Then, she would be our force."

Alexandros raised his eyebrows to the other man in a fun challenge and laughed. Then he turned his dark eyes in Athena's direction, and his gaze stroked every inch of her body before he spoke.

"I will have to find an offer you can't refuse. We already have ties that bind us, and now I look forward to exploring new options that will keep us connected."

The cryptic message swirled in her mind as she explored the possibilities of *new options*. Would these options be professional, personal, or very personal?

No, she couldn't let her mind wander into a territory where he had the upper hand. Alexandros was smooth, like a panther in disguise. And Athena hated herself for being attracted to an arrogant Greek. Even worse, to the man who'd just up the ante on her dream property and was raising the resort almost out of her reach. She needed to remain detached and professional.

"It will be a cold day beneath us before I let such an asset come your way." Luca offered comedic relief, and she attempted a nonchalant smile.

"Duly noted," Alexandros said, allowing Athena to retrieve her hand while looking from her to Luca. "I have one more *industry* question before we settle down to enjoy the evening."

"Anything, my friend," Luca said.

"Why the sudden interest in Greece? Not that Strintzaris minds the competition, but Giardetti's play for the property in Crete surprised me."

Holding her breath, Athena wondered how Alexandros would react to the truth. Her gaze skirted toward her boss, who didn't reveal anything more than required. Luca simply shrugged.

"We both know it has a certain appeal, good potential, and the timing is right. Now come, let's catch up." The Italian indicated a seat, inviting his friend to join them for a drink. "I'd love to put business aside for an hour or so."

"Certainly."

Sitting back in the leather antique wing chair, Alexandros placed one long leg across his opposite knee, drawing a slight glance from Athena. This was a man very comfortable in his own skin. Warm, sun-drenched skin covered with the world's best clothing.

"My staff assures me the symposium is a great success. They are looking forward to tonight's closing festivities. And of course, I could not have missed the fundraiser you hold so dear, Luca."

Shifting in her seat, Athena interjected in a pleasant and professional voice. "We are happy to hear that, Mr. Strintzaris. Your staff is delightful, but your generosity will be the most effective tonight. The Naples Children's Charity is a worthy cause, and the funds raised this evening will be allocated toward a home for children waiting to be adopted by loving families."

"Undoubtedly, a worthy cause. I look forward to contributing in any way needed. In any way," he emphasized, causing the flame deep inside her to flare up.

When he turned back to his friend, Athena tucked a strand of hair behind her ear with uncertain hands. She couldn't decide what to make of the powerful Alexandros Strintzaris. Known for being a ruthless businessman, he was now friendly and supportive despite the recent clash of interests in the Cretan property. Alexandros' next question confused her further.

"Luca, where are we with the monetary situation? Will we need Strintzaris Enterprises to fund half the project?"

"No, no, we will save your name and influence for a different time," said Luca. "Between us, tonight will exceed the amount necessary for the home. We'll surpass our projected goals. Miss Lakis has single handedly secured the most generous donations from our industry." He awarded her a proud smile. "It seems that no one is able to refuse or minimize her requests."

"I know I never could," Alexandros added.

It was her turn to raise a mocking eyebrow and smile. "Duly noted. Now if you gentlemen will excuse me, I have a ball to attend."

Both men stood as she left the lounge.

Alexandros watched Athena's departing form, loving the way her tight suit skirt swayed with each step. His friend's hand on his shoulder guided him to sit, and Alexandros turned his attention back to Lucas.

"Something you care to discuss?" Lucas asked. "Perhaps our magnificent Miss Lakis?"

"No. I know who Miss Lakis is. I just didn't know how much more I'd like to know her." He blew out his breath with a low whistle. Letting his hands express deeper feelings, Alexandros gestured in a repetitive circular pattern while he spoke. "She is rather intriguing."

"Don't let her pretty face fool you. She's a remarkable and shrewd businessperson."

"I don't doubt that, but I was speaking more on a personal level. She has close ties to my family, yet she does not bother to contact me about a donation. I would have doubled any request she made." Alexandros motioned to the waiter for drinks.

"Give her more credit. Besides, she knew you'd be here tonight if it were necessary. Don't feel cheated. Your eyes will have their fill of her at the ball. She organized a very successful event this week, and you know that I am not very easy to please."

Luca looked directly at Alexandros and leaned forward, placing his elbow on his knees. "To answer your next question, our relationship is strictly professional."

"I know," Alexandros said, nodding his head confidently.

"And how could you be sure your sources are correct? Are your ties that strong?"

"They are," he replied as he leveled a focused gaze his friend's way. "Now stop trying to make me dance to your tune, and tell me what you have been doing with yourself. How is that lovely young bride you keep locked away at a Boston university?"

Chapter Two

Alexandros leaned against the cold marble column and watched Athena meticulously entice each person during her thirty-minute presentation on the children's home.

"Because of your generosity, children facing an at-risk future will have a safe place to call home, a place in which to feel secure. We will not allow the tumultuous events that bring these young ones to us to follow them into adulthood. The children will only know the love and care in which this haven will be run, and they will feel *your* love that has made such a place a reality."

Applause resonated in the hall. Athena smiled and raised a dainty hand to acknowledge a few of the guests individually. Working from left to right, she recognized over twenty sponsors, each one beaming with pride from her attention.

"I would like to thank Luca Giardetti for conceiving the idea for the children's home, and honoring me with the opportunity to contribute some of *my* love." She turned and walked to where her employer stood. Taking his hands in hers, she kissed his cheeks. "Thank you, Luca, for allowing me to work on this. It is the greatest gift I've ever received."

Everyone in the room cheered, and applause rang out again. Luca hugged her, took a bow, and then kissed both her hands. As the other man's lips touched her skin, a shot of possessiveness rammed Alexandros in the gut. It was too cozy, too intimate.

Damn, she was chummy with her boss. If she wanted a man to give her projects so she could shine, *he* could do it. Athena could work for and thank him. And he wasn't married.

She wiped a tear from the corner of her eye before returning to the podium. "The warmth that fills this room is only the beginning. Thank you, everyone, for your support. Please enjoy the ball."

He could see Athena was in her element. Knowing more than just the fund-raising side of selling an idea, she was a master marketer and financial analyst in one enticing package. Carrying herself like a veteran model on a Paris catwalk, Athena left the stage and glided across the ballroom acknowledging each of the sponsors, but one. Him.

Confident and brilliant, she was the brightest star of the night. She seemed completely unaware of her affect on the room's male population. If the amount of gazes following her every move indicated this appeal, then she appealed to both married and unmarried men alike.

Alexandros grinned smugly. Eventually, he'd have this amazing creature for his own. It didn't matter if she was avoiding him at all cost, she'd change her mind.

She was incredible. Her long lean body had just the right amount of curves, especially from the angle she afforded him throughout the night, her rear.

Occasionally he stole a look at the sparkling brown eyes, or caught a glimpse of her dazzling smile as it flashed across her golden face and her lips shimmered with sensuality. What he wouldn't give to enjoy that view on a daily basis.

Why hadn't she approached him yet?

He would find a spot for her in his organization in a heartbeat. She could be a great addition to the Strintzaris team. Instead, she worked for the competition.

Then it hit him. Maybe, just maybe, it was because of the personal connection that she chose to work for Giardetti. She didn't seem like a woman who would pull strings, namely by approaching his brother, to land a job.

Well, now that Alexandros had met her, she wouldn't have to approach his brother. He'd find the way to bring her to his side. Professionally, and perhaps with a few personal benefits when the time was right.

Memorizing each of her visible features and fantasizing about the ones concealed by her cream silk gown, Alexandros was more intrigued by this woman than any woman he'd met before. Helen of Troy could not have tempted him more.

Erotic scenes of covering her body with his own as he tasted the sweetness of her mouth danced in his head. The image of settling between her thighs and claiming her forever had him turning his back on the party to pull his jacket across the front of his body in order to preserve a decent appearance.

Forever? Was he out of his mind? He was not the forever type of man. He liked playing the field, and he'd never made a commitment to any of his lovers. One day he'd settle down, but that was one day, not now.

Kicking himself, he reminded his libido that Athena was not a woman he could play with. The close friendship she maintained with his brother negated the typical rules of a simple romantic tryst. Alexandros would have to control the physical temptation. He was stronger than it was.

Since he needed to establish a friendly and professional relationship with her, he would keep her close by, at least for the time being.

The maître d' approached Athena and whispered something in her ear. She nodded and took the phone from him, indicating to the guests to excuse her.

Athena couldn't wait to tell Tony about the fundraiser's success. The evening had turned out even better than anticipated, and she stepped out on the terrace to relish the triumph in private.

"Hey, Tony. Glad you called."

Her brother's laughter preceded the conversation. "I thought you might need rescuing from a garlicky-breath suitor just about now."

"Not yet. Thanks for the concern, but I think I can handle myself."

"Yeah, but you'll always be my baby sis. So tell me, how is everything going there?"

"Better than I ever could have hoped," she said, elated at the night's events. After giving her brother all the details, she assured him she'd try to fly to London and have dinner with him the next night, and then she rang off.

Placing the phone on one of the cocktail tables, she walked the length of the balcony, enjoying the clear sky and cool spring breeze of the night.

A deep masculine voice sounded behind her, shattering her solitude. "You're an extraordinarily talented and beautiful woman, Athena. Did I mention you look like a true Greek goddess tonight?"

Heat burned her cheeks and she turned to face Alexandros. She'd avoided looking into his sultry eyes all evening, only to find herself on a moonlit terrace, the single recipient of his searing attention.

Dropping her gaze to his strong Grecian nose, then to the sure line of his lips and the defined jaw that met his proud chin, she could not deny he was a very good-looking man. He radiated strength and confidence in every step.

Taking a deep breath, she reminded herself that not only was he standing between her and her future, but men such as Alexandros were emotionally off limits to her. No matter how tempting, she had vowed not to become involved with his type. She would never risk the humiliation of a broken heart again.

"Mr. Strintzaris, I hope you're enjoying the ball." She pressed her hands to her stomach. "I would like to thank you personally for your very generous contribution."

Whom was she trying to fool, speaking to him in this cool manner?

He removed his jacket and gently wrapped it around her shoulders. "It's a little chilly. You're shivering."

Was he that dense to believe the sweet night air had made her shiver, or was he looking for an excuse to come near her? Either way, accepting the jacket put him in very close proximity. The jacket retained his body heat and his scent. Athena settled into it.

She gasped when he leaned forward and brushed back a tendril of hair that blew across her face. The chemistry between them was exceptional, something she had never experienced before. Still, she took a step back. Intimidated by her own delight in his closeness, she wasn't sure how to respond.

"Athena, why have you been avoiding me?"

Overwhelmed by his ardor, she inched further away. "Excuse me, Mr. Strintzaris?"

"Alexandros. Call me Alexandros. You know our relationship is more than calling me Mr. Strintzaris. We are practically related. Yet, you do not contact me about a donation, and you do not approach me tonight. You have been avoiding me." His dark eyes said more than his controlled words.

"You're a friend of Mr. Giardetti. There was no need for me to approach you."

"I'm your best friend's future brother-in-law." He stepped closer to her, but didn't touch her. "Or have you forgotten that Heather is engaged to a certain Costa Strintzaris, who just happens to be my brother?"

Allowing a few inches between them in the balcony's shadows, his gaze settled on hers, but he didn't wait for her to respond. "In less than a month, we will jointly witness Costa and Heather's marriage. We'll be their *koumbaroi.* I'm the best man, and you're the maid of honor. I think I deserve to be on a first name basis with you, *koukla mou,*" he finished with a term of possessive endearment in his native tongue.

"It's best to keep tonight on a professional level." She pulled his jacket closed. This meeting was doing things to her body she'd rather keep concealed.

"No, it's not *best*. Professional is not enough."

"Costa and Heather send their regards," Athena relayed mechanically after a long pause.

"I'm sure the message wasn't so unfeeling and cold. In Greek, we say love and kisses." He lowered his intense gaze to her lips, adding with a husky undertone, "And you are a Greek. You know better."

She struggled to maintain her composure as he stared at her mouth.

"If you want me to go, just say so," he breathed against her lips.

Her mouth betrayed her protesting mind as it opened, and leaning forward, she touched her lips to his. Alexandros sealed their kiss, and their bodies came into intimate contact, setting fires deep inside her.

Automatically, she snaked her arms around his neck and invited him to taste. He pressed harder, exploring her warmth with experienced vigor in the art of pleasuring. Drawing her hips tighter against him, he fueled the flames.

Gently cupping her face in his hands, his thumb stroked her trembling lower lip, and he looked deep into her eyes. Athena held his gaze as she smoothed her gown against her and then removed his hands from her face in a slow deliberate move.

"Alexandros, I'm working here. Please."

"Tomorrow then, once your work here is done," he said, replacing the jacket that had slipped during their kiss back around her shoulders.

Typical, arrogant man! What made him believe she'd spend her free time with him? He hadn't even bothered to ask. Rather he'd told her how things were going to be.

She did not argue, she simply allowed him to guide her into the ballroom. "We can't mention this again." She reluctantly removed his jacket and handed it to him. "The kiss, the conversation...it was inappropriate."

He grinned, placed a friendship style kiss on her cheek, and dropped his hand from the small of her back. She flashed him a courteous smile and returned to the guests.

Chapter Three

Athena returned to the confines of her suite, thrilled that the ball had been a fantastic success. Exhausted, she fell onto the couch with a sigh, imagining what Alexandros was doing at the exact moment. Was he thinking about her? If he was, his thoughts were probably focused on how easily her meek defenses had crumbled.

She'd been powerless to resist him. All common sense fled the moment his lips touched hers, leaving her vulnerable to his seductive assault. What was happening to her? Where was the iron will she lived by when she needed it?

He was so far out of her romantic circle. Experienced, nonchalant, and extremely confident in his appeal to others. What made him think she would welcome his advances?

That was the problem with Greek playboys. They were so smooth, so attractive. Possessing the ability to make you the center of the universe, even if it only lasted for a short time. Playboys were dangerous. They were sure to tire of you and move on to the next woman. Athena could not trust a Greek. They enjoyed the chase more than the results, and she'd never let herself become romantically involved with one.

Watching other women make fools of themselves was not her only deterrent. She had witnessed only two weddings that were the result of these relationships, but she had seen many more end as nothing but a mere fling.

Sharing her first kiss with a Greek boy had proved to be devastating, and contributed the most weight to her mistrust. It wasn't the kiss, but the fact that he had humiliated her in front of her family. She'd fallen apart and her brother had designated himself to settle the incident. Losing control of the situation was the harm.

Okay, enough about Greeks; enough about Alexandros. Enough romance for the night. Just think that he is ready to snatch the resort from your hands. The resort you've worked so hard for, the resort you've promised the next three years of your life to.

No, nothing would come between her and her goal. Not even the powerful and mighty Alexandros Strintzaris, no matter how debonair or tempting he may be.

Despite her resolve, she went to bed thinking of him and it kept her awake. Turning continuously in the large bed, she kept fluffing her pillows to get comfortable. The down comforter tangled around her legs and she kicked it off.

He had tasted so good, so addictive. She could still feel his arms holding her possessively, still feel the warmth of his jacket and smell the scent of his cologne. She let out a longing sigh, and then tossed her pillow across the room.

She needed to stop the Alexandros thoughts!

Soon he would be Heather's brother-in-law. She would be spending a lot of time with him in Santorini before the wedding, and she didn't need to complicate things with romantic feelings. His brother was her close friend and his brother's fiancé was the best friend she'd ever had. She would not jeopardize her relationship with either of them for a fling with Alexandros.

Knowing his family history, his business genius, and now his physical potency, didn't help. Rather, it terrified her.

Overwhelmed by the memory of his body pressed against hers, she realized he was her ultimate nightmare: a Greek playboy she may not be able to resist. She needed to distance herself, and put things into the proper perspective.

The phone rang at the perfect moment. Grateful for the distraction, she smiled as she reached for the receiver and heard her oldest brother's voice.

"Demo, how are you?"

"I'm good. Listen, Strintzaris just upped the bid half a million. Are you sure you want to continue with Luca's deal?" Her brother's voice was impatient. Obviously, he didn't think it necessary for the negotiations to take such a turn.

Athena calculated the new terms. They would make things more difficult, but they were within her grasp. "If they only went up half a million, they're preparing to stop. Round up to the next level and we'll be done. Point out the fact that the beach is public and won't belong to the resort. The county could cut off the resort's access at any time. They did that in Platania with the new luxury place next to Thea's. Didn't we hear a rumor about the same happening here?"

Demo sighed into the phone. "Athena, let me fund the buy. The property is worth much more than we're at now, and–"

"No! I won't let you do for me. I'm perfectly capable of completing this deal on my own. The time of the big, strong Greek man taking care of the little woman has passed. I don't need Daddy, Tony, or you to pave the road for a good husband to do the same."

"That's not what I think, or what I meant. And you know that. It makes a–"

"I said no. Go up a full million, and they'll stop. If they really wanted the property, it would be out of my reach by now. Aren't you the one that said it's worth ten more?"

"Yes. However, I've never known Strintzaris to back away from something he wants."

She pictured Alexandros in the boardroom. Tough, determined, refusing to yield. "I could see that." She sighed. "I met him tonight. He's impressive and very persuasive."

"Strintzaris is in Naples?"

"Uh-huh. He and Luca are good friends. Alexandros came to support the children's charity."

Demo's tone changed from legal advisor to big brother. "Don't forget who he is. Don't look at him as Costa's brother. Alexandros Strintzaris is your competition and nothing less than a shark."

"DDGC! I know."

"What do you mean?"

Athena smiled and felt a tingle run through her. *Drop Dead Gorgeous Competition.* "Nothing. Don't worry about me. I'm not fickle. Negotiate the deal, Demo. Get me that resort."

"Good girl. I love you, sis."

"I love you. *Kalinihta*, Demo."

At nine the next morning, Alexandros rang the front desk and asked to be connected to Athena's suite. However, he was politely told that Miss Lakis was not available. She had an early flight and had left for the airport at six. The desk attendant said Miss Lakis had requested room service for him before leaving, and it would be brought to his suite.

Moments later, he opened the door to accept a tray containing a demitasse cup of Greek coffee, a plate of feta cheese with olives and some bread. He looked at the breakfast and smiled. Yes, he was correct about this woman. Not only was she thoughtful, she was also complex, alluring, smart, beautiful, and most of all, perfect for him.

Athena may have steered clear of him this morning, but she had unknowingly, intuitively, left her door open to him. By acknowledging who he was, and providing what he liked, she'd made an effort not to offend him. Even while she avoided being alone with him.

He knew she sensed the intensity of what they'd shared, her body had told him. He remembered her arms around his neck and the brush of her fingers as they'd caressed the hair above his collar. Her dazzling eyes had searched for strength to pull away from him. Aware of the waver in her step as they re-entered the ballroom, he too had hesitated to let go of her and break the physical connection. But she'd been correct; she was working.

He knew better than to pursue her in a business setting. She was too much of a professional to allow it. However, if he had not placed immediate distance between them, he would have given in to his desires and found some way to take her to his bed.

Forget it. You can't approach this woman that way. Gain her trust through friendship, and possibly establish a professional relationship. You could hire her for real. The idea held vast appeal. She'd be near, but he would not need to promise anything that he couldn't deliver.

Alexandros picked up the small cream-colored envelope propped against the flower vase. He flipped it between his fingers and wondered what she would write, instead of telling him in person. He peeled the gold seal and pulled out the card with the pretty handwriting scrolled across it like a poem.

Alexandros,

Sorry I missed you

—had an early flight.

It was a pleasure meeting you.

Looking forward to the wedding.

See you in Santorini.

In friendship,

Athena

"In friendship? You can think that for now," he said. Grinning, he read the card again. Realizing the irony of her actions, he knew she was fooling only herself.

"Our time will come, *koukla mou.*"

Chapter Four

A symphony of red, orange, and deep purple guided the jet containing Athena and her two best friends, Heather and Costa, in their cloudless decent.

Athena turned to Heather and squeezed her hand. "Are you ready for your *pethera,* your mother in-law?" she asked in concern for the other woman's feelings.

"No, but I will be. All those horrid interrogation stories about Greek mothers must be greatly exaggerated."

"Let me tell you, my *Americanaki*, you are the envy of the single Greek female population. Costa comes from a family held in very high esteem within the Hellenic business community. Many parents have prepared their daughters dowries and offered them shamelessly with no success. But, and here is the big *but*, Anna Strintzaris prays both her sons will be as lucky as she was and marry for love, not for future prosperity. You have love on your side, Heather. Stand your ground, be your true self, and I am sure that Mrs. Strintzaris will love you."

Athena held onto Heather's hand to give her strength. It was funny how she had the answers for her friend, but she could never allow herself to trust in love, especially not with a Greek. Costa was an exception, just like her brothers. He was one of her best friends.

But his brother, Alexandros, was an arrogant, extremely good looking, and dangerous Greek. Her stomach did a flip at the thought of seeing him again.

Gently leaning her head against the seat, Athena closed her eyes and attempted to clear her mind of him. She looked at her college roommate, her best friend. The two had been inseparable from the first minute they'd met, and Athena wanted this week to be perfect for Heather.

After graduation, Athena had spent the summer in her parents' homeland. It was then that she'd met Costa in Mykonos. They had become instant friends, spending many afternoons sharing *frappes* and long talks by the beach. He'd taken on an older brother role and insisted she needed to wise up to the ways of *xeni*, foreigners, vacationing in Mykonos.

"You owe me," she had said to Heather on their weekly phone call. "I've spent my summer vacation finding you the most eligible bachelor in Greece!"

"So you keep him and stop match making." Heather had laughed into the phone.

"He's perfect for you! I know what I'm talking about," Athena had insisted. "He's coming to New York for graduate work and you'll see for yourself."

"You come to New York so that I can see you for myself. The summer is not as fun on the island of Manhattan as it is on the

Greek islands. I can't wait until we sit on MacDougal Street and enjoy our usual *shawarma*. Just think of all the yummy meat in that toasty pita with *tahini* sauce, instead of your Greek *tzatsiki*. Okay, you like your gyro, but I miss you. Hurry back."

The friends shared that *shawarma* the Friday before Labor Day, with the addition of Costa. He claimed the *shawarma* held nothing to the Greek gyro and told Heather he would bring her to Greece so she could taste test for herself.

The day had arrived.

Athena looked out the little window, watching the sun dip behind the horizon. The Santorini sunset was world famous, and now she could see why. The colors painting the sky were mesmerizing. She sighed softly as she sat back in her seat.

"Hey, I should be the one that's worried. Do you want to talk about it?" Heather asked.

"No, I'm fine. I just want this week to be perfect for you."

"It will be for me," Heather leaned closer, whispering in her friend's ear. "Perhaps it will be for you, too. Alexandros is very hard to resist and it seems you two have a definite attraction. Do me a favor, forget your rule and listen to your heart for once."

Athena squeezed her eyes shut again. She prayed that Costa's family would not see Heather as an outsider, and she prayed for her own sanity. Perhaps business would keep Alexandros at a distance, and away from her.

The jet touched down and coasted on the runway, then taxied toward a shiny gray Mercedes parked next to a red motorcycle. There were three figures standing beside them.

The friends descended the plane's stairs, and Costa stepped forward to engulf the awaiting threesome. His father, Spiro, mother Anna, and brother Alexandros.

"I've brought you the best gift, a *kori*! The daughter you have always wanted." Costa urged Heather forward.

The matriarch of the powerful Greek family had a twinkle dancing in her eyes. Reaching out her long gracious arms, Anna took Heather into her embrace. "Welcome, Heather, we are so happy to have you in our family. I've been counting the days to your arrival, *kori mou.*"

"Me too, Mrs. Strintzaris—" Heather began.

"No! None of that!" Anna waved a dismissive hand. "*Mama,* my child. You are to be my son's wife. The two of you will become one. He addresses me as *Mama*, and so shall you, *kori mou.*"

Tears gathered in Heather's eyes. "It will be an honor to call you *Mama.* I haven't called anyone mother since I lost my parents. Thank you."

"Okay, Anna, enough, you are making the girl cry. Come, *kori mou*, it is my turn to kiss my son's bride." Spiro took Heather into his large arms and softly whispered into her ear, "You call me *Baba.*" He thrust a large bouquet of roses into her arms, and bent to place a kiss on her forehead.

Next in line was Alexandros, the tallest of the three men, and a younger version of his handsome father. He opened his muscular embrace to Heather and grinned.

"Costa makes my life so difficult. I will have to beat all the island's single men to keep them from trying to change your mind about marrying my brother." He sealed the family's reception with a kiss on each of her cheeks.

The older couple welcomed Athena warmly with her own set of kisses and flowers. The family accepted her friend, but she could not relax. She still had to greet the man whose gaze scorched her skin. She dared to glance toward him. Alexandros seemed like a boy about to devour his favorite ice cream cone.

It was unavoidable. He was unavoidable.

Heather returned to Costa's arms, and Athena inched to the end of the line. She prayed that Alexandros would stop looking at her with those hypnotic eyes, but her prayers went unheard.

"I am most pleased to see you again." He took her hands, raised them gingerly to his burning lips, and placed a slow tender kiss on the inside of each wrist.

Athena's heart jumped, as his deep voice filled her ears. Her skin sizzled where his lips had caressed it, and she found herself sinking into the almond-shaped abyss of his eyes.

On this heavenly island, he wore no tuxedo and no business suit, only a simple pair of khaki linen pants and a crisp white shirt open at the collar to reveal the tanned skin underneath. He looked like a normal man—a normal man who happened to fit all her physical fantasies. And without the suit to present him as a business associate, or more accurately as her rival, he was now only DDG. The Competition lost in this island paradise.

Her gaze trapped, she could not look away from his face so close to hers. His tanned, chiseled cheekbones, strong sun-kissed nose, and fiery lips were framed by hair like luscious, chocolate waves in which Athena wanted to soothe her hands.

She lost her voice and could only smile back.

"It is okay." Alexandros leaned in and spoke in a whisper. "I feel it too. We will discuss this later, in private."

Athena jerked her hands away. Yes, Alexandros was the most beautiful man she had ever seen. Yes, he made her heart jump. Yes, his touch set her skin on fire. Nevertheless, who did he think he was? Perhaps she didn't want to be in *private* with him.

Gathering her strength, she took two steps back. She had not expected to see him so soon. This was going to be a tough week.

Alexandros placed the suitcases in the trunk and threw the Ducatti's keys to his younger brother. Costa, in turn, placed a red helmet over Heather's blonde head, climbed onto the impressive red motorcycle, and patted the space behind him for his fiancé. "Time to properly introduce you to Santorini."

Baba Strintzaris opened a rear door for his wife and scooted her over before nestling beside her.

"Athena, you ride up front with me," Alexandros announced.

"Your mother will be more comfortable up front."

"You're a stronger person than I if you can separate those two. Come on, *koukla mou*, let's go."

Hearing him call her his doll again was very unsettling. Just as his relaxed, easy manner was difficult to handle. Hesitating, Athena stepped into the car and found herself too close to him. It was a luxury vehicle, but on an island like Santorini, size mattered. Too big wasn't good.

But as Alexandros guided the car smoothly along the hairpin turns, she relaxed, losing herself in the rugged beauty.

Spiro, a graceful back-seat tour guide, identified the different towns and told Athena of their history. Rows of towering cliffs jutted against the dark magenta sky and reflected off the deep azure sea. Blue domes crowned the little white homes scattered on the rugged cliffs creating quaint villages.

Another turn and the fabled black volcano, which some believed had sunk the ancient civilization of Atlantis, was on their right. The sun set into the sea, its descent filling the sky with amazing streaks of orange and red. Promising to toast any barefoot visitor's toes, the sand on the beach below was a scorching black.

Lost in the beauty, Athena was stunned when an arm whipped out and held her back on the seat. A large truck headed straight at them. She grabbed at the muscle on his forearm.

"*Thee mou*. My God," she gasped.

Alexandros maneuvered the car right to the edge of the cliff, and the truck sped by them without incident.

Wetting her dry lips, she closed her eyes and tried to calm her palpitating heart.

His hand lightly stroked her knee. "I've got you. I will not let anything happen to you. Now breathe for me."

Athena found herself releasing her breath. She believed him.

The butterflies left her stomach and fluttered straight to her head. Why did this man have such an effect on her?

It's only the jetlag wreaking havoc on your senses. Stop projecting romantic feelings toward Alexandros, or you will regret it.

He was obviously a man who always got what he wanted, and women continuously fell at his feet. She'd heard the stories about him gallivanting all over the Greek islands as a teenager, leaving countless broken hearts in his wake.

Now he was a grown man and dangerous to her. Above all, she could not deny the electric charge his touch sent through her body.

Athena had a rule, and during her many summers spent in Greece, she had never broken it. She would not get romantically involved with any Greek. No summer romance for her. She had seen these islands flood with vacationers looking for a tryst each summer and had no desire to join their ranks.

Well aware of how women craved the attentions of men such as Alexandros and Costa, she had made a conscious decision not to be influenced. She always made friends, as she had with Costa. She laughed and socialized by day, but slept alone each night. She had no plans of changing her rule any time soon, and especially not now.

A notorious playboy, Alexandros continually graced the pages of the gossip papers. Last month, he'd headlined with a blonde French model on a yacht. She was sunbathing topless, and he was standing behind her applying lotion to her back when the paparazzi snapped the picture.

Costa had laughed when he'd seen the paper. "When he falls, he'll fall hard, harder than the rest of us. He hasn't met the right woman yet."

If that were true, she'd thought, it sure wasn't from lack of trying. Alexandros was young, handsome, and rich, topping the list of most eligible Europeans each year. He never had any shortage of women vying for his attention. A Greek golden boy, he had grown his father's lucrative shipping enterprise and had expanded into the international hospitality industry.

Most importantly, he was Costa's brother, soon to be Heather's brother-in-law. Athena could not allow herself to make any mistakes that would ruin her relationship with her friends, and simultaneously get her heart broken. Heather and Costa held a very special place in her heart and she planned to keep them in her life for many years to come.

She moved her knees toward the passenger door and out of his reach. She shouldn't feel at ease with his touch. No, no touching.

Chapter Five

The car arrived at *Villa Kalithea,* and Athena realized they stood on the Caldera. A shiver ran down her spine as she looked over the volcano's edge. The part of the island that had broken off from the volcano had an addicting, raw beauty and smelled of danger.

The Strintzaris house was not a little home with a blue dome. It sprawled across the edge of the dark cliff, its numerous domes still gleamed in the fading light, and its many verandas promised visitors a spectacular view. Massive bougainvillea climbed the white walls that reflected the warmth out to sea. She could not see the vibrant colors of the flowers in the dusk's dim light, but Athena could smell the heavy, seductive scent of jasmine in the evening air.

Waves crash on the jagged rocks below, then retreated, caught up in their never-ending dance of give and take. This place had a pulse of its own. Lulled by its warmth, she was awestruck by its strength and intense beauty. Santorini captured one with her many sensual gifts and made it impossible to leave her behind. It gripped fiercely at Athena's fundamental nature as her feet moved slowly beneath her.

Roses lining the walk grabbed her attention and she bent to smell them. Lovingly cupping a large bloom, she stroked the velvety petals and inhaled its musky, sweet scent.

Mr. and Mrs. Strintzaris walked ahead, leaving her alone with Alexandros.

"Your home is exquisite."

"Thank you, I'm glad you like it," said the voice belonging to the man who'd occupied her mind the past weeks.

"I can't believe it's only a summer place. I'm surprised your parents don't live here all the time."

"We built *Kalithea* five years ago, and it has since become our base on the island. I like it because it's on the Caldera and the view is fantastic. Hence the name, *Kalithea*, or *good view*." He shrugged his broad shoulders. "Baba's house is inland. Mama and Baba use both homes, depending on their mood. They are funny that way."

Anna and Spiro had reached the main entrance, and signaled for Alexandros to take a phone call. They motioned for Athena to join them for fruit.

Sitting on the patio, Athena enjoyed the sweetest watermelon she'd ever tasted. It was from the villa's garden and cut just before the family headed to the airport.

"I am very glad we finally get to know you," the older woman said to Athena. "My sons have had the pleasure of your company and speak so highly of you."

"The pleasure is mutual. I know Costa well, he's been one of my best friends these past few years, but I've just recently met Alexandros."

"Perhaps you made a bigger impression on him. He talks about you often."

Like such a man could fail to impress her!

Meeting him had sent quakes through her body and soul, an event not likely to be forgotten.

When Alexandros returned from inside the house, his mother asked him to clarify the issue.

"No Mother, we didn't have the opportunity to get to know each other well, or personally." He turned to face Athena. "It's too bad you had such an early flight in Naples last month. We missed each other a second time. You were out to dinner with Costa last week, and I arrived to the restaurant as you were stepping into a taxi. I guess the third time is the charm." His lips curled into a smile as he tapped his finger on the table.

"I, for one, am very happy we have this time together," Anna added. "You've been a big part of Costa's life and our Heather regards you as a sister. Even though they complain that since you started working for Luca, you barely have a social life."

"I guess they're correct." Athena shrugged. "I love my work, and I seem to let it carry me away at times. No offense, since Strintzaris is now in the hospitality business, but I feel very privileged to be learning from one of the oldest and most highly regarded dynasties in the industry. Giardetti International is a great wealth of information."

"Yes, especially since Luca's marriage brought about the merger of two power houses within the industry," Alexandros said. "Their international presence is immense. Giardetti is doing very well, but they've slowed their growth in order to revamp some of their existing sites. I'm surprised Luca is interested in Greece and the Cretan property at this time."

"We are. The property in Crete is a prime location and has the potential to be a true-five star resort." Athena shifted uncomfortably in her chair, wondering if her boss had told the handsome competition it was really she who wanted the resort. She was the one who had made the decision to outbid Alexandros and was determined to take the property right from his hands.

"True," he affirmed. "And you seem to have a great deal of influence in this project."

"Perhaps that is why Costa and Heather complain. I'm trying to learn as much as possible during the time I spend there, and I sometimes forget the simple pleasures. Like enjoying an afternoon with my friends."

The older woman tsked her disapproval. "*Ohi, kori mou.* You can't live to work. You must enjoy your life and ...how is it the Americans say? Work to live?"

Alexandros' gaze narrowed as he sat back in his seat, flipping his blue and silver *komboloi* between his fingers.

Athena wondered what stress the worry beads were supposed to relieve.

Leaning his elbows on his knees, he flipped the *komboloi* again and spoke to her in a low voice. "Are you aware of the situation allowing Giardetti to be such a giant in the luxury hotel industry? Has Luca discussed it with you?"

"Yes, he has. Obviously, you know, too, or you would not have asked about it. However, that is his personal matter. I don't think we should discuss it any further."

Alexandros nodded and sat back in his seat. "I agree. I simply wanted to be sure you know the facts and are not misled in anyway."

His protective tone surprised Athena. Letting her guard down for a moment, she thanked him for his concern. She was well aware that Luca's marriage was only on paper. Her boss had married his dying best friend's sister in order to protect the young woman's assets from unsavory characters until she was old enough to run the empire she had inherited.

The conversation changed to the wedding festivities, and after snacking on the fresh fruit and cheese, Athena found herself checking the time. A small yawn escaped her lips.

Mama Strintzaris chuckled and said, "I'm sure the long flight was tiring, *kori mou*. Why don't I show you to your room so you can rest? It's almost ten, and you'll probably sleep through the night."

"That sounds lovely, but Costa and Heather haven't arrived. Should we be worried?"

"They've arrived." Anna took the younger woman by the hand and led her to the railing. "Look at the home on the left."

Athena's heart skipped at the sight of the beautiful illuminated villa. "It's extraordinary. It shares *Kalithea's* view, which is such a fitting name, because I don't think I've ever seen a better view in my life."

"It sure does. That is *Villa Cardia Mou*, and fitting with that name, it is Heather's wedding present from Costa. She has captured *his heart*. If you look carefully, you can see them on the second story terrace."

Athena smiled as she made out the two figures on the balcony.

"Now off you go. You need to sleep. Alexandros will bring your things in a bit. It's the first room up the stairs, on your right. Have a good rest."

After thanking her hosts, she climbed the stairs to her room. The heavy wooden door swung open, and Athena immediately noted that it was larger than her New York apartment. A king size mahogany bed dressed in crisp white linen sheets and a white hand made crocheted blanket with doves invited a weary traveler to rest. Matching crochet curtains adorned each of the windows and the closed door at the far right. The masculine mahogany desk belonged in a decorator's showroom and emanated strength and vitality. She walked into the luxurious en suite bath with its marble tub and the sink positioned below a window overlooking the volcano.

Like a little girl, or a princess in a fairytale, she pirouetted out of the bathroom and into the solid muscle of Alexandros' chest. An electric current streamed through her body as she came to rest against him.

"Sorry, I didn't mean to startle you," he said in an accent that drawled sensually on each vowel. "The door was open and I called out to you, but you did not answer."

His hands remained on her hips where they had gripped to steady her. His eyes devoured her, his scent wafted throughout the room, and he filled the large space, making it feel small.

"I take it you are happy with your accommodations? Let me show you the best part."
Thankfully, he released her hips and placed a leading palm on her elbow.

She nodded, feeling him consume all the oxygen in the room. His touch set her arm on fire as he guided her past the little kitchenette and the table for two. They passed the sitting area, where Athena could lose herself in a book for hours, and he pulled back the white curtains. Opening the French doors, he stepped out into a veranda where a free shaped infinity pool melted into the sea.

"From here you can hear the volcano hissing its song. It inspires and refreshes me when I need to think."

"I can see how. It is breathtaking."

"You are breathtaking," he said, as his gaze slowly moved across her. "You belong here. A true beauty, free and strong. Just like this place."

He came closer, and the heat between them tantalized her senses. He took her chin in his fingers raising her face to his. "For such a strong and determined woman, you're suddenly very quiet."

"Determined women aren't necessarily chatter boxes." She shifted her weight to her heels, arching her body a few inches back from him.

"True, and you could never be accused being such a thing. You barely talk to me. Why?" Alexandros inched forward and paused for a moment.

His close proximity engulfed her, and she wanted to immerse herself in him. Flames flared in her core, and she could feel her face grow warm.

"It was very unfortunate we were not able to get to know each other better in Naples," Alexandros said in a low voice.

She sealed her gaze to his and lifted her determined chin high in the air. "Yes it was. However, it was unavoidable. You know—business." It was a lame attempt to avoid further conversation on the eventful evening.

"Athena, you're very good at what you do. Your *business* doesn't control you. *You* command *it*. Even if that wasn't the case, there is a lot more to life than work." His words were rich with challenge.

"Thank you for the kind words," she said, refusing to give his undertone any credence. "I'm sure this vacation will revitalize me. I'm looking forward to relaxing and refreshing this week."

His lips curved into a knowing grin. "You've successfully managed to avoid my question. I think your actions clearly answer it instead."

She searched for the correct words. Her tongue found the roof of her mouth, and traversed the curve inside her teeth. She swallowed to moisten her scratchy throat.

The air crackled and a cool breeze wrapped around her ankles, grounding her feet, making her feel balanced. Her stomach settled, and she unexpectedly breathed with ease. She was surprised to find comfort that words didn't need to express her emotions. It wasn't necessary for her to implicate herself.

For the first time in her life, she didn't mind loosening her grip on control and letting someone else take the lead. It was out of character, but she allowed herself simply to be in the moment of time, not to act or react.

His thumb stroked the line of her jaw, and he spoke softly. "I'm looking forward to having coffee together in the morning. Thankfully, there are no early flights. *Kalinihta.*"

His lips lightly brushed hers, before moving to settle on her cheek. He let her go, and walked inside to the desk. Retrieving his laptop and two files from the second drawer, he strode out of the room.

She watched him close the door and realized there was no chance for rest here. This was his room, his desk, and worst of all, his bed.

Why had he given her his bedroom? The villa had six other bedrooms she could have used.

Heat filled her cheeks at the thought that this was his bachelor pad. The place he seduced his women away from the family. Is that why his favorite part was the side door to the terrace?

There was no reason for her to be jealous, but she was. After all, Alexandros was simply flirting, and here she was becoming possessive. She needed to rest; jet lag was obviously clouding her common sense.

Turning on the water for a bath, she began to empty her suitcase into the wardrobe as the tub filled. When she was done, she submerged herself into the fragrant water and let her stress melt away. The warm bath accentuated how tired her body was, and she longed for the tempting bed that called to her. Athena stepped out and quickly toweled off. After laying a dry towel on the pillow, she climbed between the sheets.

Sleep consumed her immediately.

Athena was here, sitting in his house, on his island. She was not going to get away this time. He had to play his cards very carefully. He had one week to learn what she was hiding from him and to make her trust him.

She would not go back to work closely with his influential friend on a different continent. Luca may be married, but Alexandros knew he was not faithful. Besides, what man could resist the desire to claim a woman like Athena? Luca had the advantage of her trust and loyalty, but nothing past that at the moment. Alexandros would be damned if he allowed the opportunity for anything further to develop.

Most importantly, Alexandros had fate on his side.

Athena had come to him now, regardless of the reasons. She would be more comfortable, more accepting, if she thought she was here on her own terms. She could not, would not, leave as she came.

His brother had said she was very committed to her work and did not have a love interest at the time. Alexandros would see to it that she did not have time for one at all. If only he was able to convince her to work with him, he could control his feelings and his libido. Then he would have time to learn what made Athena tick.

He smiled as he closed the door behind him, but couldn't help thinking in primitive terms. Perhaps this woman was too much to keep at arms length. He might need to rethink his course of action and help speed the timetable up. His head fell back against the door and he relished the thought.

"You will not sleep alone in my bed for much longer, *koukla mou.*"

Chapter Six

Athena awoke, rested and recharged. The sun was going to rise soon, and she loved to watch the first light of day color the sky.

Pulling back the sheets, she got out of the warm bed and strolled into the bathroom to wash the sleep out of her eyes. She grabbed the pink linen robe hanging on the door, needing protection from the crisp morning air, and tied it around her waist as she walked onto the veranda.

Taking a few steps out, she stopped, seeing Alexandros sitting at a little round, blue table under one of her windows. It was stacked high with newspapers and his coffee sat on the edge.

He looked up from the newspaper he was reading and gave her a lazy smile. "*Kalimera,* you're an early riser."

"Good morning to you."

Playing with his *komboloi,* he motioned for her to join him. "Hope you slept well."

She would not admit to sleeping well, with him visiting her dreams all night long. She had enjoyed the dreams and had hesitated to put an end to them. But he did not need to know that.

"I haven't slept a full eight hours in years. It was nice for a change."

"Good." His eyes shone with approval of her tousled morning look. "This is the best reading spot in the house. Have a seat, and I'll get you some coffee."

"I was hoping to see the sunrise," she replied, remaining in the doorway and not taking a single step toward him.

"Not at this angle, this is where it sets." He neatly folded the paper and placed the blue and silver-chained beads on it. "Come," he said, rising from his chair.

He led her around the house to the east. "The sun rose a few minutes ago, but it will be coming over that mountain momentarily."

They stood waiting quietly, and the sun made its appearance over the mountain Alexandros had pointed out. The warm, colorful rays spread across the gray sky, shedding light on the valley between the two mountains.

Donkeys called loudly to each other, a rooster sang his song, and birds left the trees to spread their wings in acrobatic feats. The island was coming awake, and the animals were playing their part. The trees took on their green moist hues and the bougainvilleas radiated a rich red color.

Enjoying the smell of morning, she inhaled deeply. A sense of renewal filled her soul and she smiled at the sensation. The air was crisp, refreshing and contained the mystery of things to come. "What newspapers do you have?"

"Greek, English, French, and American. Take your pick."
They talked softly as they walked around the house.

"Would you like coffee?" he offered.

Athena nodded.

They walked into the kitchen. She found the *briki*, while he took out the smooth brown powder and the sugar. She poured water into the stainless steel coffee pot, which looked like a tiny pitcher with a long black handle, and then turned to take the spoon and coffee from him. She placed two heaping teaspoons of coffee into the warm water.

"Sweet?"

She nodded, and he dropped the sugar in. She slowly stirred the mixture to a gentle boil and as it began to rise, then turned to pour it into the demitasse cups he held on the tray of breakfast cookies.

She went to the sink, rinsed the *briki* before grabbing some napkins and following him back outside. She noted how naturally they moved around each other in the kitchen, and grinned.

At the table, they each sat in one of the two chairs, and picked their respective papers. Alexandros decided she needed her space, and made a very conscious effort not to touch her.

It was working. She twirled a long finger in her curls as she read. Occasionally, she would stop playing with her hair, pick up her coffee and sip. Placing the small coffee cup down, she'd go back to twirling those long strands, a different one each time, and then more reading.

The situation tormented him, tested his self-control. He wanted to run his whole hand through those enticing curls, but for now, he'd simply watch her, allow her time to assimilate him into her space.

Alexandros had considered setting up a business transaction to see her after Naples, but quickly decided that would have been futile. She did not mix business with pleasure.

An obstacle he could easily overcome. Too bad the other hurdle would not be so easy. His brother had shared a bit of knowledge about Athena. He'd told Alexandros that she was adamantly opposed to becoming involved with a Greek.

The thought outraged him. He was a Greek!

Moreover, why was a Greek not good enough for her? Was he not proud? Was he not loyal? Greeks had history. A fierce and passionate line of ancestry ran through his veins, and hers.

Yet she refused a personal attachment to a Greek.

"Did you see this?" Taking a deep breath, he pointed to an article about Giardetti International's most recent actions toward purchasing the resort in Crete. "It says you're giving us a 'run for the money'."

"Yes, I know." Her gaze narrowed and she shuttered her eyes. "I don't think we should ruin the week by discussing business."

"I don't see it as a problem, but if you do—"

"I do." She dropped the paper on the table, crossed her arms, and turned her back to him.

Interesting. Maybe the problem between us is business and not personal. That is easy to fix.

Picking up his coffee cup, he took a long, noisy sip, eyeing the tension on her shoulders.

Definitely, work related. What a shame.

He resumed reading.

After they had traded all the papers, he stretched out his legs and casually reached over to tap her hand. "What are your plans for today?"

"Since I'm the maid of honor, I need to see what Heather wants to do. I know she and Costa have a few wedding errands, so I will probably do some work by the pool while they are gone. You?"

"I have some meetings to attend. The last one around three o' clock with an associate from the States. Would you like to go the beach or to a café afterwards?" He asked politely, keeping with his initial plan to win her trust.

"It sounds nice, let's see how the day goes," she offered, failing to commit.

"Good," he said, looking at his watch. "I have a meeting soon. See you later then." He stood and walked away.

Athena cringed at the awkward end to their breakfast together.

Why had he left so suddenly like that? Did he really have a meeting or had she insulted him? He had been a perfect gentleman all morning. Nothing like her vision of a spoiled playboy.

"What is wrong with me?" Athena whispered under her breath.

She had enjoyed reading the paper with him, taking the time to be herself. Not needing to entertain him, she'd found it easy to relax.

Hoping for an afternoon on the beach, she went to her room to dress.

After considering her options, Athena chose to spend the remainder of the morning walking the estate and pruning roses she found on the south side of the house.

Taking into consideration the time difference with New York, she returned to the little blue table with her laptop and logged onto her email for the latest update on the resort. She had made her final bid just before boarding the Strintzaris jet. If Alexandros surpassed it, she'd be out. Her dream of building the first Athena Resort would not begin in Crete.

Maneuvering the computer so the sun wouldn't hit the screen, Athena clicked for her mail and held her breath. Tony had emailed her twenty minutes ago, Demo ten. She opened Demo's since it was the most recent.

Yia sou, koukla! I'm in Zurich, so call my cell. D.

That was it? She was going to strangle him. Athena opened Tony's email because it would be faster that getting her phone from inside the room.

Morning, koukla. Call Demo on his cell. He has news. T.

"I'm going to kill you both!" She hurried inside and dumped the contents of her bag on the bed. Grabbing her cell phone, she cursed under her breath when there was no signal. She didn't want to use the house phone. Not when it was DDGC's phone. She'd go and pick up a local SIM card.

Shoving the phone into her shorts pocket, she walked out to the veranda and was about to hustle down the stairs when the phone rang. She stepped back up.

"*Ne?*" Yes, she answered.

"Hi, *koukla*. Did you get my email?"

"Demo! Yes. And I'm going to kill you for keeping me waiting." Feeling her legs grow weak, she returned to the table and sat. "Tell me, please tell me."

"You did it, baby sis! The resort is yours, debt and all. Congratulations!"

"Yes! Yes! Yes!" She leapt from the chair and did a happy jig, jumping up on each syllable.

Demo laughed into the phone. "Hey, is that anyway for the owner and CEO of the latest player in the luxury hotel industry to behave?"

One more jump. "Yes!"

She joined her brother in laughter and dropped back into the chair. "Wow, Demo."

He chuckled and teased her, "Athena, you'll have to be a bit more articulate in your new position."

"Thank you, Demo. Thanks for all your work on this." She blew a kiss into the phone. "I know you think I'm doing this all wrong, but I really wanted to do it on my own."

"I'm proud of you." Demo paused, and she caught her breath. "I would have done it the same way. I just wanted it to be easier for you and I wanted to help. Just promise me that you'll come to Tony and me if you need us."

"I promise." She raised a fist in triumph and kicked her feet. Smiling she asked for the rest of the details.

"Sammy has delivered the personal contract between you and Luca to his office. She'll be faxing it to me later tonight. Giardetti should be transferring the remainder of the money into escrow as we speak, and the resort is preparing an executive bungalow for your arrival."

"Yes!"

"Athena," he warned jokingly. "More articulate!"

"Yes!" she repeated and laughed. Taking a deep breath, she listened to the rest.

"They'll operate until the end of the month. Then the Giardetti flag will assume control. So take your well-earned vacation and enjoy the wedding."

She sobered fast. "Why did Alexandros stop?"

"We don't know, and we don't care. Things like this happen every day."

She dropped her head to her hand and whispered into the phone. "What am I supposed to tell him?"

"Nothing. Athena, you need to separate business and pleasure. That is why you pay us the big bucks. We run interference and you don't need to come face to face with the adversary. Alexandros is your best friend's brother-in-law. That's it."

She hesitated. How did she explain how wonderful the family was?

Demo let out a heavy breath. "Listen, Alexandros makes and breaks deals like this on a daily basis. He's a professional, and I hate to sound flip, but he doesn't see it the way you do."

"I know," she conceded. She'd been working with Luca for five years and had seen him do the same. To her, this was not just a good investment. It was the cornerstone of her future.

"Stay with the story that we've come up with for the press. That way you don't lie to friends—and you'll achieve your goals. The resort's reputation has to be rebuilt under the Giardetti name to have a chance to compete in today's cutthroat market. It's a win-win situation for everybody."

"You're right." Her mind and her stomach dueled for her attention. Logic eventually gained the upper hand. "I guess I'll enjoy everything here and let business wait. After all, that's what you guys do every day."

"Exactly. Don't confuse the two."

Chapter Seven

Athena worked for two hours on the Cretan hotel's marketing file before Alexandros came into view, speaking into his headset.

"No... fair market value," she heard as he made a gesture to ask if she was hungry. She smiled back and mouthed a silent "no" as he walked by.

Still talking, he sauntered over to the pool and slowly sat on the edge. His hands moved, expressing the urgency of the point he made to who ever was on the other end of the phone. His broad shoulders relaxed as he placed his bare feet into the pool and leaned over to draw on the water with his finger. She regretted saying no to him. If she had said yes, she could go sit with him. Magnetically drawn to him, her feet moved without consulting her mind.

He was nodding his head and concluding the call when he looked back at her. She continued, slowly walking to where he sat. He smiled, and took off the headphone and patted the spot next to him.

"Come and have a seat."

"This is a nice setting to conduct business." She searched for something else to say as she took off her sandals.

"It sure is, but life isn't just about working. It is time for a break." Looking up at the mid-day sun, he stretched his arms and pulled off his simple white t-shirt, then dove into the pool.

She felt a hot trickle running down her back as he surfaced, exposing his muscular chest and defined abdomen.

"Where is everyone?" he asked.

"Your parents went to see your grandmother. Heather and Costa went to lunch with Gianni Poulos and his wife, and I stayed behind to do some work."

He simply nodded and did a few laps in the pool. She watched as his powerful arms cut into the water, his long legs only needing a few kicks to get him from one side to the other.

When he turned on his back, her gaze followed the line from the soft, dark hair on his chest, down his sculpted abdomen, into the wet red cloth clinging to his manliness.

Her mouth went dry as she saw his long, broad outline. She forced her eyes to move to his thick thighs and down his legs before looking back to his beautifully masculine face. If they pictured him in the marketing material for the hotel in Crete, they would never have a vacancy. His body was so male, so strapping, so tempting.

She had to stop these thoughts. Her brain said she wanted nothing from Alexandros but friendship. Her body was obviously not listening. Water splashed onto her hot face.

"Come in," he said, spraying her again.

"I need to change into a bathing suit." She got to her feet as he hauled himself out beside her.

"As you are." He laughed, grabbed her waist, and hurled them together into the deep end.

His arms closed around her as they resurfaced and gently pushed her hair out of her eyes. She liked the feel of his arms more each time he held her.

"You're stunning. If you appear in a tiny bikini, I can't promise to behave."

His hand cupped the back of her head and pulled her closer, kissing the top of her forehead. Suddenly, he released her completely, and moved to arms' length.

"It's a lot easier to behave if you're wearing a NY Knicks basketball t-shirt," he said with a spectacular grin. "Come on, a five lap race—loser does the lunch dishes."

She inhaled deeply and began to swim, thankful for the diversion. She was a strong swimmer, matching his strokes, and releasing the sexual tension that had swelled her chest. On the last lap, he pulled ahead. He would not be doing the dishes.

Lifting himself out of the pool, he stood on the white stone and went over to the house. He pulled two towels through the bathroom window, and walked back, placing one by the poolside for her before drying off himself.

"Thank you," she said walking out of the pool.

Her shirt hugged her body, revealing a little bit of skin above her shorts. She tugged at the clinging material. His gaze made the wet skin on her abdomen tingle. Grumbling a curse under his breath in Greek, something about damming the Knicks, he started to walk toward the back of the house.

"I'll get lunch," he said. "Change and meet me in the kitchen."

How could a simple request sound like a command when Alexandros Strintzaris spoke? He was so confident, insisting on what he wanted. Surprising herself, she was a willing recipient of his simple request. She wanted to spend more time with him, and she found his self-assuredness intriguing.

Under the shower, her skin was very sensitive to the drops of water. Her body was betraying her. It wanted more of Alexandros, more than friendship. Well, she was a sensible woman and good sense dictated that she wanted only friendship. Stepping out of the shower, she talked to the woman in the mirror.

"He said *he* could behave. So can you. You only have to be with him for a week. Control yourself. Do you really think he'd find you attractive if he knew that you were the one outbidding him in Crete? You and not Giardetti?"

She dried herself, pulled on a simple white tank dress and went to the kitchen to meet him for lunch.

There was a large Greek salad and a loaf of crunchy bread on the kitchen table. Alexandros poured two glasses of wine and offered her a seat.

"I hope you're not too hungry. This is the extent of my culinary skill."

"It looks great. Thanks," she said taking the wine.

He appeared preoccupied as they ate. She watched his eyes grow dark and his eyebrows come together.

"Anything wrong?" she asked when he finished his wine in one swig.

"I was thinking about something related to work," he replied.

"Can I help? I type, file, and make coffee."

"Really funny," he said, raising his gaze to her. "Thanks, but no. I need Costa to handle it. I know he is caught up in the wedding preparations, but I don't want this to keep. I need him to do it today. Did they say when they were coming back?"

"No, but Heather's jetlag is bad. I know she wants to nap this afternoon. It shouldn't be long."

"Good. I have that three o'clock conference soon, and then I can talk to him."

"Go on, then. Get ready for your call and let me finish up here. After all, I let you win the race."

"Thank you," he said, giving her a light kiss on the cheek. "You really are a sweet doll, a true Greek-American *koukla,* letting me win and all."

Quickly, she cleaned up and went to her bed for an afternoon siesta. Her head on the soft pillow, she thought of Alexandros.

He wasn't the narcissistic playboy she had expected. He was nice. She liked him. And her feelings for him were becoming much more than friendly.

Voices crept into Athena's sleep. She slowly climbed out of bed, wrapped the sheet around her, and looked out the window.

"Sleeping Beauty is up!" Costa said, sitting just five meters away from her door. The brothers lounged on the patio, enjoying tall glasses of iced coffee. "Come join us".

She dressed in a pair of khaki shorts and a white cotton tank top, brushed her teeth, put on some mascara, and pulled her curls into a high ponytail. She slipped her feet into her favorite sandals, and stepped outside to join the men.

"Heather is sleeping," Costa said. "I think she might sleep through the night. Baba and Mama should be up soon. You know how we Greeks need to 'refresh' for the night ahead."

"Oh yes," she replied. "When I was little I used to fight my mother every afternoon. I never wanted to sleep. When I was a teenager, I looked forward to the siestas because we used to stay out all hours of the night. Now, I crave the luxury after a long morning of crunching numbers at work. Too bad Wall Street doesn't see the need for a siesta."

"A sweet *frappe* to awaken your senses?" Alexandros had been sitting in silence until then.

"Yes, thank you. I would love one."

He unfolded his long legs and rose from his seat. He hovered over the others for a few moments, shifting his weight from left to right like he was weighing something in his mind. His arms locked behind his back, he looked off toward the sea before addressing Costa.

"Any questions? You know what to do?"

His brother "tsk'd" pensively and tilted his head upward indicating negative, no questions.

"I want it done when I return." Alexandros turned and strode off.

Athena instinctively knew it was connected with what had upset him at lunch. Whatever it was, it must be very important to him.

"Business. Don't fret," Costa said, in an evident attempt to diffuse the tension.

The friends enjoyed small talk for a few minutes and then she carefully asked the question that had nagged at her since her arrival the previous night.

"*Cardia Mou* is the most beautiful name for your new villa. It's fantastic. Don't misunderstand my question Costa, but isn't *Kalithe*a large enough for the whole family to vacation here?"

"Of course it is," Costa agreed. "But *Kalithea* is Alexandros'. It's not my parent's home. He built this place for his family. I built *Cardia Mou* for Heather."

Alexandros returned. He placed the *frappe* and a snack of *koulourakia*, her favorite cookies, in front of Athena.

"Thank you," she said, smiling at the attention he appeared to enjoy giving her. "I didn't know business tycoons could be so domesticated."

Costa smirked and nearly choked on his drink.

Alexandros simply returned her smile, ignoring his brother. "There's a time for everything. It's nice to make you smile, *koukla mou*."

Then Alexandros turned to his younger brother and his temperament changed. The smile faded, his dark eyes glared, and he handed his cellular to Costa. "Finish this. I'm tired of the drama."

Costa walked away from the table and spoke to someone on the phone. His shoulders stiff, his gate calculated, he circled around the pool. When he approached the table again, his jaw was set in a hard clench, the vein by his temple pulsed, but his eyes told a sad story.

Anna had joined them during the conversation. Staring from one son to the other, she asked what was wrong.

"Once again, envy has shown her greedy face," Alexandros began. "Giorgios can't stop wanting what doesn't belong to him. He is back to his old tricks and habits again. I'm sure gambling and drinking are the least of it.

"Giorgios has been funneling company funds into a personal account, and he had the gall to try to frame our Costa. We were investigating the transactions before he came to me and loyally informed me that Costa was stealing from the company."

"*Thee mou*," the matron of the family whispered in devastation.

"I gave him the rope, and he hung himself, Mother." Alexandros let out a long breath before continuing, the anger vivid in his face. "It has been almost a month that the snake thinks he has come between Costa and myself. I thought it appropriate for Costa to tell him his plan failed."

Nodding, Costa sat beside his mother and took her hand in his. "Giorgios began to whine and give me a story about his gambling debts. He had put his mother's, Thea's, house into the pot of a poker game and lost. He'll never learn!"

"*I* will buy Thea's house and pay his debt." Alexandros' voice boomed. "She can live out her old age there. He's not to set foot in our homes again."

"He's clearing out his office as we speak."

"Good riddance!"

Costa raked his fingers through his blonde hair as he offered some clarification to Athena. "Giorgios is the son of Baba's late brother, Taso. When Theo Taso passed away, Baba felt responsible for his brother's family. Thea and the children came to live with us in Athens. Our homes shared a backyard, and we all grew up together. Eleni was only a baby and we would fight to push her stroller around the yard."

The brothers took turns relating the history for Athena's benefit. "We played on the same soccer teams," Costas continued. "We had our first drinks together, and studied for the university entrance exams together."

"During university," Alexandros said. "Giorgio developed a drinking problem. We searched the streets for him all hours of the night, not aware of his gambling until he went to Baba and asked him to pay his debt. That was the first time he'd wagered Thea's island home." His jaw squared, his Adam's apple protruding, there was no mistaking the agitation growing in Alexandros' voice as he relayed the history.

"Baba gave him the money on the condition that Giorgio would enter a rehabilitation program. He did, and he completed it. After university, he worked in the accounting department of the company."

"He isn't effective in a corporate environment, regardless of the help we all offer him." Alexandros reached for his *komboloi* from the table. Flipping it over between his fingers, he shook his head, and looked out at the sea.

Costas frowned. "He's very good with numbers, but doesn't have any people skills. He thinks he's above others. We've kept him employed as an accountant for one of the ships. He can't handle more than that."

"Now he has proven that he cannot do that either!" Alexandros' voice flooded with fury.

"It is so sad, *paidi mou*," Anna said. "Once you were like brothers. The three princes and princess Eleni. Why does he want to drive a wedge between you?" Tears rimmed the matriarch's eyes. "Perhaps he can enter a rehabilitation program again."

"I told him that was the only way we wouldn't press charges. He agreed," Costa informed his older brother.

"Thea and Eleni are, and always will be, welcomed. But not Giorgios. I'm done with him," Alexandros proclaimed.

Discussion closed.

Suddenly Athena felt like she was eavesdropping and excused herself.

"Please, *kori mou*, don't feel awkward. Its better we resolve this issue before worse things happen. We have nothing to hide, and you're definitely not intruding," Anna insisted.

"It's okay. I just want to walk along the cliffs and watch the sunset," she replied.

"I will escort you," Alexandros said. He stood, claiming he too needed a change of scenery.

Chapter Eight

Athena felt her stomach leap into her throat. She'd put herself in a more difficult predicament than she was in before. Being alone with Alexandros in the most romantic place on earth at dusk, and witnessing one of the most beautiful sunsets in the world, was not what she'd had in mind.

She was a rabbit placed on a dog track. What had she done?

The walk began silently and continued casually with Alexandros asking about Athena's family.

"My parents, Nikos and Maria, are originally from Crete. They were childhood sweethearts who'd decided to move to New York as soon as they were married. It was difficult at first, because Dad couldn't practice medicine until he passed the boards in the States."

"What type of specialty does your father practice?"

"Dad is an ophthalmologist. And yes, we all have 20/20 vision," she added. "I also have two very smart and handsome brothers, Demo and Tony. They're much like you and Costa. Our home was full love and laughter. I have always known how blessed

I am, especially in comparison to many of my friends who do not have such close families."

"You were born in New York, but you have no accent when you speak Greek," he remarked.

"We went to Sunday school and Greek school twice a week. We ate dinner together every night, unless Dad had an emergency. All through the winters, we supported each other in our mutual sporting events and then usually spent our summers in Greece with the rest of the family."

"That's a good thing. Your summers in Greece brought you to us. You met Costa in Mykonos."

She nodded. "I graduated from NYU, and as you know, I've been working for Giardetti since."

"Brains and beauty, a combination for success in the international hotel business," he said.

"It helps that I took French in school." Embarrassed, she avoided the compliment. "I have the advantage of being fluent in three languages. Now tell me something I don't know about your family."

Relief flowed though her body when he seemed inclined to maintain their present course of conversation. If they kept talking about the families, she could stop thinking about how his musky scent was surrounding her.

Alexandros smiled and started to speak in Greek. "How far back to you want me to go?"

"When your parents met."

"How about we climb down here, sit on the beach and enjoy the sunset while we talk?"

"Sure." She took his outstretched hand for balance as they climbed down the *monopati*, a narrow little dirt path littered with stones, on the steep cliff. He wrapped his long fingers around her hand and put his body ahead of hers. Almost immediately, she regretted not wearing her sneakers and stopped talking in order to concentrate on her footing.

Without saying a word, Alexandros guided her over the well-worn path. When they were on the beach, he turned, placed one arm behind her knees and carried her. She looked into his dark brooding eyes as he took matters—and her—into his own protective hands.

"There are many loose rocks in this area. I don't need you to fall or sprain an ankle," he remarked, as if he did this sort of thing every day. She was about to protest when he added, "I should have realized you weren't wearing sneakers."

"Well thanks for the concern, but I think I'm a little too big to be carried."

"I'm bigger, and this seems to be a perfect fit," he argued, continuing across the expanse of black sand.

Alexandros balanced her on his knee and took off her sandals. He then placed her feet on the sand. Athena decided to let it go and change the subject.

"It's so warm," she said. "The weather has begun to cool off, but this sand is just a pinch off hot."

"It's black volcanic sand. It demands the sun's attention all day long, so it's always warm. However, the breeze from the sea which is at a much lower temperature, and has cooled considerably since noon," he replied, unbuttoning his shirt in a sensual motion that had her concentrating on every movement.

Athena's eyes burned as he pulled the shirt open and slid his arms from the sleeves.

Not again, please!

His tanned sculpted chest was broader from this angle. His jeans rested perfectly on his hips, and were worn in all the right places. Her mouth went dry and she found it hard to concentrate.

He flicked the shirt and laid it on the sand. "Come, have a seat."

Athena hesitated, staring at him as if she was looking at an alien, but she took his hand and allowed him to guide her to his makeshift blanket. He sat behind her, stretching out a long muscular leg on either side of her body. Alexandros wrapped an arm around her waist, entwining the other in her curls as he guided her head to rest on his chest.

His clean male scent intoxicated her. Turning to face him, she felt dizzy as her cheek brushed against his chest. It took her a moment to remember what she needed to say.

"I may have given you the wrong impression," she said quietly. "But I have a rule, and I don't do this."

"Do what? What rule?" he asked, smoothing her hair behind her ear.

"I don't get romantically involved with Greeks on my summer vacation. I never have, and I don't plan on becoming a notch in someone's belt this year."

"You could never be a simple notch in anyone's belt, especially not my belt." His lyrical voice almost lulled her nerves to a gentle hum. "Just relax, *koukla mou,* and enjoy the sunset. I promise I won't do anything you don't want."

That was the problem. She wanted to lose control with him, to let her sensible, responsible side take a break so she could join the party.

She laid her head back against his sculpted chest in silent turmoil. They watched the concert the sun put on for them, and she felt him relax against her.

Red and orange flames danced across the sky in harmony with the large ball of fire. As the ball touched the water's edge, the flames began to sizzle and the sky took on a magenta hue. When the sun dipped beneath the horizon for the night, the smoldering embers continued to float about the dark blue sky.

"This is surreal. It feels like we are suspended in time," she said.

A groan came from low in Alexandros' throat. "It means we can leave everything behind and begin again tomorrow. We can choose to start fresh, or we can build on what we have. I want to begin something new." With his fingers, he lifted her face to his and grinned. "Do you really think I'm smart and handsome, as you said earlier?"

"I said that?" Her ears rang in alarm.

"Yes, you did. You said you had two really smart and handsome brothers, just like Costa and me."

She made a quick decision. "Yes, you are."

His strong-bronzed thumb lifted her chin to him. She could feel his breath on her lips.

"In that case, you should finish kissing me."

"Finish? I never kissed you." Her tongue flicked nervously on her upper lip as he dropped his gaze to her mouth.

"You certainly did, right before you slept in my bed." He was playing with words, she knew it, but a tingle traveled up her spine nonetheless.

"You kissed me."

"So don't you think it would be rude if you didn't kiss me back?"

When she didn't respond, he lowered his mouth to hers. Her lips parted in acceptance, taking him in. His tongue traced every corner of her mouth like a boy enjoying his ice cream, stirring heat deep within her core. Passionate lips traveled down her neck.

For all it was worth, time stopped and she was suspended in this beautiful scene. Alexandros locked his arms tightly around her, lay back and pulled her onto him. He took her face in his hands, and placed a slow kiss on each eyelid. Kissing her nose, the dimple on her chin, he covered every inch of her face before his lips caressed the sensitive spot behind her ear.

She heard a wave crash on the surf. Her mind cleared for a single moment, and she pulled away.

"No, I will not be a notch in your belt."

He stopped and looked at her closely. His eyes narrowed, and she wanted to shrink into her skin. He would think she was a tease. Why did she even come here with him?

"What do you mean?" he asked. A tear escaped her eyes and dropped on his cheek. "Don't cry, *agape mou*, no tears. I will not hurt you. You can't possibly think I would?"

"I believe you don't want to intentionally hurt me, but you could."

"I know good things are worth waiting for." He held her close, stroking her hair in slow, gentle motions. "I don't want you to be scared to be with me, I want you to be happy and proud of being with me. We will take this slow, but if we don't risk, we will never know what we could have."

She was confused. He didn't sound like the piranha she envisioned a moment ago. No longer able to look at him, she lowered her eyes. "Thank you for understanding."

"No, I wouldn't say I understand. I just don't want you upset. It is purely selfish. I want you happy. I want you to know you want me, the way that I want you."

"It's not a matter of want," she said, in a small voice.

"I'm not going away," he warned, smoothing her hair. "I'm just giving you a chance to get used to having me with you. I'm very hard to shake off you know."

They sat quietly watching the stars together. When hunger became an issue, they began the walk back to the family. This time they traveled a little further down the beach and took the stairs Spiro had built up the cliff.

They reached the top, and Athena reminded him of their original conversation. "You still haven't told me about your family and parents."

"Dad built his own shipping lines from a single boat he won in a card game while he was in the navy. He argued with his lieutenant that the game had gotten out of hand and there was no need for him to collect any winnings, but being a man of his word, the lieutenant had insisted that Dad must collect his winnings or he would insult his honor. He did, but he has never again placed a bet on a card game."

Alexandros placed a possessive arm over her shoulders, pulling her to him as the chilled darkness settled around them. Her skin was hot beneath his touch, despite the cool breeze. The corners of his mouth turned up in a smile. She was starting to accept him.

His obvious need for this woman astonished him, and he couldn't understand why he couldn't control it as he did every other aspect of his life. Frankly, he didn't care. He just wanted her with him, needed to feel her against him.

He pulled her a little closer and continued with his story. "Baba's service in the navy ended three months later. He found himself with a boat, a shrewd mind for business, and a heart full of ambition. He was, and still is, a workaholic. It was said he never took a holiday until he was thirty years old and had thirty boats in his fleet. He christened the first transatlantic vessel in his fleet after the lieutenant who gave him his start: Argyris I."

"What about your mother?" she asked.

"I'm getting to that." He laughed. "The first holiday Dad took, he came back to Santorini. His family lived in a small farming village twenty kilometers from Fira, the islands capital. The village was celebrating his visit at the square when he saw her for the first time.

"Baba swears he could not break the enchanting hold her eyes had on his and he asked permission to see her again. They were married a month later."

"And then along came you?"

"Yes, two days after their first wedding anniversary. Costa was born two years after that."

They entered the veranda and greeted the family.

The other two couples didn't comment on Alexandros' possessive hold, rather they poured everyone some wine and raised their glasses.

"*Gia Mas*! Cheers!"

Chapter Nine

It was almost noon. Athena stretched her body across the bed and felt the energy flow to each of her limbs. There was a longing inside her that she had never experienced before. It grew stronger as she felt herself searching the sheets, looking across the room, and listening for Alexandros. She smiled and pictured him lying next to her, pictured giving herself to him.

A grown woman who rarely indulged in fantasies, Athena was more traditional than she cared to admit. It wasn't that she believed she needed to be a virgin on her wedding night, but she wanted her first time to be more than simply special.

She'd seen men enjoy the chase, talk about their conquests, and forget them once they were out of sight. Too proud to have her name spoken in those conversations, Athena had never found anyone worthy of the risk.

Trust was a decision that didn't come easily to her. Instead, she had lived the last ten years by the 'No Summer Romance' rule. Yesterday, she had broken her rule. And in doing so, she'd had the most amazing day in recent memory.

Emotions she didn't know she was capable of feeling tightened around her heart. She enjoyed having Alexandros beside her on their walk, she dreamed of him all night, and she woke looking for him.

A warm flame began to grow deep within, and as it spread out from her heart, she decided that it couldn't hurt to enjoy the week with Alexandros. She'd be friendly, but she would control her physical desires. Minimize the attraction and therefore lessen the risk, but still indulge a bit.

Besides, she was leaving on Monday, there was no time for her to fall in love and have her heart broken. No expectation, no strings attached.

Happy with her decision, she dressed and went to find the others. It took her a few minutes to find the kitchen from the inside of the house.

"Good morning," a young woman called out in Greek when Athena arrived in the kitchen. "You must be Athena. You are as beautiful as Mr. Spiro said. My name is Stella, and I work for the Strintzarises. Mrs. Anna and Heather are on the balcony waiting for you."

"Thank you and good morning to you, too," replied Athena, in perfect Greek.

"I'm glad you speak Greek, it will make it easier for you to remember everybody at the party on Friday."

"The party?"

"Oh, yes. The whole family is anxious to meet Costa's bride. Mr. Spiro had to fight to keep them away yesterday so that you could rest. There is no way he could make them wait until the wedding. Besides there are so many of them and it will take some time to put the names to the faces. The party will help. Why don't you go out to the balcony, and I'll bring you coffee and some breakfast?"

"I can help."

"No, please. Mrs. Anna and your friend are waiting for you. I will not be long," Stella insisted.

"Thank you. Coffee always tastes better when someone else makes it for you." Athena smiled and walked out to the other women. They were sitting in a shaded area, but the sun's heat reflected back at them from the rest of the patio.

"*Kalimera, kori mou,*" said Anna.

"*Kalimera*" replied Athena, as she bent to kiss both women. "What are we looking at?"

Heather eagerly welcomed her friend and started to point out the family pictures in the album she held. The pictures included five-year-old Costa on a donkey led by Alexandros through the town's cobble stoned streets, the whole family in front of a Christmas tree with the Acropolis in the background, and her absolute favorite of Costa wearing his chocolate cake on his third birthday.

Stella appeared with a tray of fresh bread, cheeses, olives and coffee for each woman to enjoy. They sat and chatted like lifelong friends losing track of time.

"I wish my mother was here with us," Athena said to the older woman. "I've been working so much lately and I don't see her as much as I should. I'd like to take time just chatting together over some coffee. She would enjoy your company."

"I hope to meet her soon. Perhaps in Crete later this summer?" Anna suggested. "What are your parents' names?"

"Maria and Nikos. Dad is from Chania, and Mom from a little village outside Rethymno."

How did Anna know her parents were from Crete? Athena had not told her. Alexandros must have discussed her with his family. He was the only one that knew. She had never even mentioned it to Costa or Heather.

Athena felt like a heel. She wanted to tell the other women her news about the resort. Such developments were supposed to be celebrated, not hidden. She wanted to share her joy. But at what expense? She had won the bidding against Alexandros. Was she being two-faced by enjoying his family's company?

"We have the equivalent of the Greek Bridal Shower today," Heather said, her words laced with happiness. "At seven, all the single women will come to the house and make the wedding bed. They will 'shower' it with gold coins for prosperity, sugar for a sweet life, and wheat for fertility. Isn't it a great custom? Make sure you fluff my pillows well. Friday we have a pre-wedding party to meet the rest of the family, the male part. Tonight it is only women."

Anna nodded. "Now let us talk about the family. I warn you ladies, our family is quite large. Do not worry if you cannot remember their names, simply address them as 'cousin' and you are sure to delight them."

The sound of a helicopter landing behind the villa startled Athena.

"They're back," exclaimed Heather. "They had some dealings in Athens this morning and left at daybreak. I'm glad they were able to finish early. Costa and I want to show you *Cardia Mou* today."

Father and sons strode into sight, looking very handsome as they smiled at the women at the table.

"Hey, look at these three beauties sitting on our balcony." Costa strolled over with a large grin on his face.

"I think we'll be the talk of the town if we take them out for a drink," Alexandros added.

"We will definitely grow two inches taller in everyone's eyes if we are seen with these mermaids," Spiro continued.

The women laughed. Anna puckered her lips. "Come here and greet me properly, *andra mou*," she called out to her husband.

Spiro obliged, and gave his wife a tender kiss. It was such a pleasure to watch a couple so affectionate, and clearly in love, after so many years together. It warmed Athena's heart and inspired similar aspirations for her life. She wanted a love like theirs, like her parents'. She didn't believe in the convenience of marriage, but in the love for it.

Athena feared it would be impossible to find, because she also wanted a man that would consider her a true partner. She needed to be self-sufficient, wanted to work, and knew these kind of men didn't appreciate a working woman.

Yet, she was surrounded by strong, passionate, and most of all, enigmatic men. They were so much more than she'd expected, and frankly, she did not understand them.

Amidst her thoughts, she smiled as Costa walked over to Heather, pulled her off her seat, lavished her with a big hug, and kissed her passionately.

"I hope you got enough rest last night because I have plans for us this afternoon." Alexandros looked at Athena and winked. "I need to meet some friends in town. I would really like it if you join me."

"It sounds great." She felt happy to spend time with him and away from Giardetti business. "Heather wants to show me *Cardia Mou*, and we are making the Bridal Bed tonight. Will we have the time for both your plans and the bride's bed?"

"Leave it to me. We'll be back."

"As for tonight, everything is arranged," Anna interjected. "All you have to do is be there. Spiro and I are meeting with the caterers and staff at one to finalize everything for tomorrow. Costa and Heather want to discuss the wedding menu with the caterers. So you have plenty of time."

Alexandros smiled at his mother before turning back to Athena. "Great, grab a swimsuit, and I have the rest. We'll go by *Cardia Mou* before we set out."

Athena went to her room, bypassed her bikini, thinking of what he had said yesterday, and grabbed her blue Speedo one piece. She liked being with him, she liked the way the family was together, but she was not ready to admit that she liked the idea of being on his arm.

Ten minutes later, each couple mounted a motorcycle and set off toward *Cardia Mou*. Alexandros took a sharp turn and Athena spread her fingers in a tight hold over his muscular chest.

He groaned. "All I want is you in my arms and to taste the sweetness of your lips."

"You'll have to wait on that, but right now I've got you in my arms." Athena was shocked by her own voice.

"That you do, *koukla mou*," Alexandros replied, taking another turn.

How things changed in a mere span of a few days. Now, she loved it when he called her his *doll*. Resting her chin on his shoulder, they arrived at *Cardia Mou* two minutes later. The villa was all it had promised to be.

When the friends gathered outside to part ways, Heather spoke privately to Athena. "It seems I have spent my pre-wedding days finding you the most eligible bachelor in Greece."

Athena felt the instantaneous blush and asked her best friend to stop teasing her.

"Alexandros is perfect for you!" Heather laughed and continued. "Trust me. I know what I'm talking about."

She kissed her friend good-bye. As she followed the subject of their discussion to the bike, indecision danced in Athena's head. She'd decided to have fun and forget about everything but the here and now. No work, no rules, nothing. She'd chosen to vacation on a Greek island like so many other tourists did annually. Of course, she hadn't planned to fall for Alexandros. Now the question was: was she falling too fast? Could she control it?

"The first thing we do is coffee. Okay?" Alexandros asked, as he moved forward to allow her room on the bike.

"No problem. I'm all yours for the next few hours," she said, wiggling onto the seat and feeling him inhale sharply.

They rode over the rugged beauty of the island and arrived at a little café on a black sandy beach. The owner came out to greet Alexandros, shaking his hand enthusiastically and kissing him on both cheeks.

"Athena, this is Dimitri. He and Baba grew up together and have been the best of friends since they were five."

"Pleased to meet you, young lady," said the older man, inviting them to sit at a quaint table in the shade.

"I wasn't expecting to see Alexandros till the wedding. He doesn't come by often enough, and especially not with such good looking company."

"Dimitri, if anyone can appreciate good company it's you," said Alexandros. "Please join us. I would like to talk to you, and I have brought the papers."

Alexandros ordered while they walked to the table, and their *frappes* arrived quickly. The two men caught up on town news and small talk.

Finishing their iced coffees, there was a change in the casual mood, and Alexandros suggested Athena put on her bathing suit so they could enjoy a swim before lunch. She understood his masked request and went into the café's restroom to change. She'd closed business meetings in restaurants, sporting events and even a bowling alley when the need had called for it.

She recognized this to be such a time and marveled how Alexandros was able to accomplish so many things in so little time. He multitasked like no other man she had met. First yesterday on the veranda, today business with pleasure, and he never missed a beat on what was happening around him.

It was clear that the older man loved him as a son and trusted and respected him as a businessman.

She lingered a bit longer than needed inside the restroom, giving the men a chance to finish their discussion. When she came out of the café, his eyes told her the coast was clear.

"I'm sure the papers are fine," said Dimitri.

"Have your lawyer take a look at them. Good business makes good friends," Alexandros said.

The other man nodded in agreement.

"Now, I believe my beautiful mermaid needs to go for a swim. Will you excuse us, Dimitri?"

"Of course, I don't want it to be said that I stand in the way of young love. Be sure to say goodbye before you go."

Athena tried to respond, but Alexandros silenced her with a primal possessive kiss before thanking his old friend. His hand on the small of her back, he picked up the pack and led her to the beach. Athena bit her tongue as annoyance rose within her. They continued towards the water.

"You're very arrogant, aren't you?"

"What has upset you, *agape mou*?"

"Stop it! I'm not your *agape*! I'm not your mermaid! Why did you let him talk about 'young love' like that?"

"Because, I agree with him." He shrugged and laid out a beach mat.

She was outraged. Who did he think he was, speaking for, about, and to her like that? She didn't trust men like him. They were so sure of themselves, and always got what they wanted.

"I want to go back to *Kalithea*. Right now."

"No, we're going swimming— now."

"I don't want to swim with you."

"Fine, how about I rub you some lotion on your back so you can suntan?"

"You are an insufferable chauvinist." The image of the gossip paper flashed in her mind. "You think you can do what you want with women."

She untied her wrap letting it fall at her feet, flipped her hair, and kicked sand at him as she ran into the water and away from him.

Chapter Ten

A smile formed on Alexandros' lips. He did affect her, and she cared enough to fight with him. He'd give her time to cool off and calm down. Then he would go to her.

Folding his arms over his knees, he sat and watched Athena. She may as well be a mermaid the way she moved in the crystal water. She dove under and resurfaced thirty feet away. Then again and again. She was tireless.

Very familiar with these waters, he knew she was pretty far out. They were deep, beautiful, and cold in June. She was a strong swimmer and did not seem to mind. If she overcame her stubbornness and swam in his direction, she would discover the sunken boat he wanted to show her.

She remained in the water for over half an hour when he decided it was time. She may have the staying power of a dolphin, but he had the determination of a shark.

He dove in with two pairs of goggles in his hand. Silently swimming up behind her, he surfaced and wrapped an arm around her waist.

"I am sorry if I offended you," he breathed, coming out of the water.

She tried to kick free, but he tightened his grip.

"Let me go."

"Stop acting like a child, and tell me why you are so upset. What brought about this change?"

"You brought me here to show off your masculine prowess to your friends. Do you bring all your girlfriends here to seduce them?"

He laughed, realizing she was not simply angry, but jealous. He liked that. "No, I don't. You're the first woman I've ever brought to this beach."

She remained silent and began to relax as he treaded water for both of them. She must have tired.

"Athena, I'm not going to tell you that I've never had a woman simply for the having, because I would be lying. But I promise you, I've never brought any of them to my family or to my friends."

"Convenient for you—I brought myself. I just showed up and spared you the trouble."

She trembled under his touch, and he felt guilty for pushing her too far. Contrary to appearances, she was too naïve and too sweet to play these games.

"Look at me." He turned her to face him. "I don't think of you like that. I don't want to 'show off' as you put it."

"Then why did you tell him I was yours?"

"That's very simple. Dimitri is a good man, and he really liked you. He has many, I mean many, handsome single nephews he would love for you to meet. If he knows you are with me, he won't think to introduce any of them to you." He paused and pushed a long dark curl out of her eyes. "I don't play the odds when I want something, and I don't care if you think I fix them. No one will dare to bother you if you are with me, and that is the way I like it."

"Please let me go," she whispered.

He knew he couldn't keep her with him against her will. She had to stay with him by her own choice. He released her and she moved out of arm's reach.

"Don't blame me for stacking the odds," he said. "You're the most desirable woman on this island. You will drive the men to distraction. They'll compete for your attention, making it impossible for you to enjoy yourself. I think it would be much easier if we eliminate that, and just enjoy each other's company."

"Stop talking like that. It's too much for me to hear and I'm not comfortable with it. Besides, what makes you think I wouldn't welcome their attention? Perhaps I'd enjoy it."

The thought of her 'enjoying' someone else made his blood boil. No, he couldn't see her with anyone but him. She would be his, and he didn't want to wait to be sure of the fact. He controlled his irritation and spoke softly. "I will stop talking to you like that if you let me show you why I brought you here."

He stretched his arm to her, but she didn't take his hand. Sighing, he placed the goggles on her head and asked her to follow him. He needed to trust she would.

She did.

They arrived at the sunken boat, and she let out a small gasp of pleasure as the sun reflected off the stern. They swam around with the little fish beside them, he pointed out the octopus in a dark corner.

Floating in the quiet over the water, the serenity of the view calmed the stressed air between them. She tried to put her foot down, and he grabbed her again. "Careful, you were about to step on sea urchin. They hurt."

They swam back to the beach and sat on the mat. He dropped a towel on her shoulders and sat beside her.

"So now that Giardetti has bought the property in Crete, will we be seeing more of you?"

"As you know, I'm heading the renovation and management team."

He nodded. Crete was less than an hour flight from either Athens or Santorini, just in case more time was necessary to bring her around.

Good.

Athena gazed up at him. "Why did you not continue bidding on the property?"

Her question surprised him. It was the first time she truly recognized the conflict in their professional goals.

"Something else presented itself. I have a greater interest in it, and didn't want to spread the company's resources too thin. Now, if we had you on our team, we could have done both."

She smiled before answering. "Thanks for the vote of confidence, but when I finally leave Giardetti, it will be to run my own resort. Working for Luca has been a fantastic experience, but my ultimate goal is to work for myself."

"Luca has that affect on people."

"He's been a great mentor, and Giardetti is a wealth of knowledge for a mind seeking to learn. We've had a very profitable relationship to date, and I believe it will continue to grow until the time comes for us to go our separate ways."

A streak of possessiveness ran through him. Why was she speaking so highly of the other man? He didn't know what, but there was more to this intriguing woman's relationship with his friend than what met the eye. Luca had assured him their relationship was not personal, but a feeling of unease sat in Alexandros' gut.

"What will you call your resort?" he asked, trying to sort his feelings.

"*Athena's*. Not because it's my name, but because it's a name which inspires—"

"An air of beauty, mystery, wisdom and the freedom associated with those traits. I like your choice in the name."

"Thank you." She buried her feet in the sand and wiggled her toes free.

"You have a time frame you're working within?"

"Yes, the first Athena's will surface in three and a half years. That resort will allow the expansion to the second a year later, and in the first decade of operations, we will have grown to a dozen resorts internationally."

"It's a very ambitious, but probable, plan. Do you intend to work with your family?" He was aware of her brothers' consulting firm. They were a team of talented and motivated Greek-Americans who were leaving their mark in international business transactions.

"My brothers always have input in my decisions. However, this risk is all my own. It's my personal dream, I can't ask them to put their plans on hold to follow mine. I don't doubt we will work together, but they have enough to do with their own business now."

"Consider Strintzaris Enterprises a friend and a resource. We welcome good competition; it only makes us better."

Alexandros was sincere. However, he found it amusing that his future competition might come in a sexy, tempting package.

"I'll remember that," she said. "What did you have for Dimitri?"

"Dimitri is getting too old to work so hard. His wife likes to spend the majority of the year in Athens and they only spend the summer months here. He married late in life, and they never had any children. Last month, he decided to sell this land. From the parking lot, down to the second jetty, and a kilometer inland, he also owns the beach rights." Alexandros outlined the property visually for her.

"He knew we're looking for land on Santorini to build a five star resort, so he approached my father. We were interested, but when he told us his asking price, we told him he was making a mistake. I know it sounds foolish, but I can't abuse a friend's trust. His price was far too low, and we could not in good conscience buy it at less than a fourth of its value."

"Good business makes good friends," she repeated.

"You were listening." He smiled. "To make a long story short, those were the appraisal papers. We should be breaking ground in October."

"That's nice, very nice. This is a perfect spot for a resort. I wish you much success here."

Alexandros had warned he would lure her away from Giardetti. Wondering if this project would tempt her, he envisioned her standing on a terrace, hands on her hips, overseeing the progress. He'd tossed about the idea of offering her the position of supervising the project. She'd report only to him, and she would be close to him where he could protect her. However, was that enough for him? He didn't think so.

Not prepared to start something with her in a deceitful way, he concentrated on establishing a trust between them. It was more important that she be with him personally, not professionally. Knowing that he couldn't prolong it any longer, Alexandros was determined to have her as his.

She spoke first. "Is this land the reason you didn't proceed with the property in Crete?"

"Yes. As you can imagine, Santorini holds a special place in my heart. Luca's interest in Crete surprised me though. Giardetti doesn't have any other property in Greece, and I'm curious about his sudden desire to invest in the country."

Suddenly, she seemed uneasy and that was the last thing he wanted. He wanted her comfortable with him.

"Are you hungry yet?"

"Famished" she answered. "Should we head back to *Kalithea*?"

"No, we're not done yet. One more important stop."

Alexandros pulled the motorcycle up to a comfortable little house overlooking a vineyard.

"Where is the love of my life?" he chimed, walking through the front door.

"Slaving in the kitchen for you," a voice from the back of the house replied. Moments later, a small woman bounded toward them, and he picked her up in his arms, spinning her around.

Inside, Athena slowly took in her surroundings. The house was small and neat. There were pictures of the Strintzaris family in every corner and a large painting of a couple on their wedding day. Athena could feel the pride the older woman took in the home, and she could definitely smell the scrumptious lunch she'd prepared.

"This is Yiayia Maria."

Athena smiled at the sight of the big man playing with his grandmother. She was short, petite, and looked very delicate in his arms. He put her down, and bringing his face to hers, he waited for her kiss. Yiayia kissed him loud and hard with the enthusiasm of a young girl.

"This must be Athena." The grandmother came to embrace and kiss her. "I'm so happy you two are visiting."

She motioned for them to follow and spoke to each of them in turn. "Food is ready. *Keftedes,* as you requested, just the way you like them. Give this boy some ground beef stuffed with feta, and you could rob him blind."

"Yiayia, you're giving away the family secrets."

The old woman chuckled as she walked to the back door. "Let's go sit out here, and I'll bring the salad."

She led them to the back patio for lunch. They ate, talked, and laughed. Yiayia seemed to thoroughly enjoy sharing her rich life experience with Alexandros, and they reminisced about his grandfather, Alex, who had passed away three years earlier.

They spent the afternoon with the older woman, barely realizing how fast the time passed. Together, they helped with the dishes before leaving.

"Yiayia, it has been a delicious pleasure—as always." Alexandros kissed her fingers in a flamboyant gesture, which pleased the old woman. "You need to rest before the making of the Bride's Bed, and I need to return Athena to *Kalithea.*"

"Thanks for bringing your girl by. It was nicer to meet her alone rather than with all the family and fuss of tonight. Now, you know where I am, and you can always come on your own." Her last statement was a standing invitation to Athena.

"Thank you. It's been a delightful afternoon," she responded.

"The car will be by at six. Yiayia, be ready. I love you."

The older woman's eyes shined with pride as Alexandros opened the door and led Athena out.

"Your grandmother is wonderful."

"My grandmother is a beautiful, stubborn old lady. She has been living alone since my grandfather passed away. She refuses any live-in help, refuses to go to Athens with my parents for the winter, and refuses to admit her body is not as young as her mind."

"She looks very capable. If she can manage, she should do as she pleases."

"I'm surprised I didn't get an argument about the car coming for her tonight. That was probably for your benefit." He climbed onto the motorcycle, helped Athena on behind him, and casually stroked her thigh as he continued speaking.

"I had to resort to threats before she would allow Stella to come over daily to help with the domestic chores. Even so, she usually has everything done before Stella arrives. They spend most of their time in the garden together. At least Stella checks on her when we are not on the island. I also have two families working the vines and they report to me daily."

"You worry about her, but I think she would ask for help if she needs it."

"She doesn't need to need. I can make her life easier. She turned eighty-three last Christmas. She refuses any help, and the island is secluded half the year. I wish she would stop being so mulish, but then again she is a true Strintzaris."

"She's lucky to have you."

"I'm lucky to have her," he said, waving goodbye to the smiling woman as they drove off the property.

This was getting complicated.

Athena liked what she saw—really liked it. A warm sensation spread throughout her body. It was something foreign, something unknown. It would be so much easier if he behaved like the primitive, conceited, arrogant cave dweller she had expected. Where was the man who took what he wanted, regardless the cost to others?

Alexandros Strintzaris was a ruthless executive who had doubled his father's fortune in five years. He wasn't a man who insisted on paying a friend fair market value for his property.

Alexandros Strintzaris was a jet-setting playboy who skimmed the Mediterranean waves with a different woman on each tide. He wasn't the man who spent a leisurely afternoon having lunch with his grandmother.

Who was this man taking her home? Who was this man who refused to let anyone come between him and his brother? Who was this man that caressed her thigh and sent an electric current through her body?

Moreover, why did she hold him just a little bit tighter when she thought about finding the answers to those questions?

Chapter Eleven

The *Making of the Bride's Bed* proved to be a delightful custom. Four generations of Strintzaris women gathered to initiate the latest member into their sisterhood.

Estrogen infused the very walls at *Cardia Mou* as nieces, cousins, and aunts were introduced to the bride. The bedroom looked like a garden of womanhood. Fresh flowers graced every corner of the room. Late afternoon sunshine entered through the large windows and the heavy double doors, highlighting the women moving around the room like bees in a hive.

Cousin Eleni gracefully placed a white package on the stripped bed. She invited the bride to remove the subtle streamers of ribbons and fresh flowers, revealing a delicate set of white silk sheets, complete with stunning gold embroidery. The younger women fitted the sheets on the bed before the youngest, ten year old Annoula, ceremoniously presented them with a white lace blanket crocheted by Yiayia Maria.

Only pure women, traditionally the family's virgins, were allowed to make the bed. The other women gathered around offering marital advice they had received from previous generations. It was a celebration of womanhood as they collectively decorated a bed fit for a fairy tale.

Yiayia was the first to place a little gold icon between the two pillows.

"*Kori mou*, I wish for you a life like the one I've had with my Alex." Yiayia took Heather's pale hands with her weathered knowing ones, raising them to her lips speaking with tenderness. "You hold your husband's heart in your hands. Let love guide you in keeping it sacred, allow it to flourish and your efforts will return rewards beyond your dreams."

"Thank you, Yiayia." Tears formed in Heather's eyes and some tissues magically appeared for her to dab away the moisture.

Yiayia moved aside, allowing each of the other women to have their say, and came to stand beside Athena.

Motioning her closer, she stroked Athena's hair and laid a tender kiss on her cheek. "One day soon, we'll be making your bed, *kori mou*," Yiayia whispered.

Stunned, Athena didn't know how to reply. She smiled and stared at the women placing gifts on the bed. Catching her breath, Athena saw, from the corner of her eye, Eleni coming toward her. She sighed in relief.

"I'm so glad for my cousin. They will make each other very happy. I've arranged a car to take us to Asteri, the island's newest dance club. John's wife, Maria, will be joining us as well." Eleni's eyes twinkled as she turned and walked back toward the bed.

The dance club was the trendiest on the island. The women followed the maître d', and made their way between crammed squirming bodies on the dance floor. Four unescorted women entering the club turned many heads as they were shown to their table. Champagne on ice awaited them, together with a bowl of fresh strawberries.

The islanders came to offer their good wishes as the night progressed. It was a fun and relaxed atmosphere with dancing, pleasant recollections with friends, and plans for the future.

Athena was returning from the ladies' room when she saw a man sitting at the table. The fine hairs on her body prickled a warning. There was something wrong, something she didn't like about the guy. She just didn't know what.

Obviously, her friends had invited him to their table and seemed to be enjoying his company. He had the same handsome appearance as Alexandros. Dark wavy hair that rested above his collar, strong Greek facial features, and broad muscular shoulders were obvious traits, but that was where the similarities ended. When he raised his eyes, she looked into cold darkness.

"These are the types of friends you should introduce me to," he said to Eleni. An icy shiver ran down her spine as he stood to greet her. His eyes skimmed over her dress and nodded.

"Athena, this is my brother, Giorgios," Eleni said, unaware of the devious curl forming on the man's lips.

How could this be? Giorgios was supposed to be in Athens. He was supposed to be in rehab. Did the other women know what he had done?

"Finally, we meet." Smiling wickedly, he moved toward her like a slimy snake.

Giorgios pulled out her chair and Athena lowered herself to the edge of the seat, her eyes searching the other faces for answers. Giorgios sat beside his sister and ordered more champagne. He charmed the other women, relating news from Athens and old family stories. Heather and Eleni laughed at his jokes, but Athena could not relax. The darkness his eyes belied his apparent sincerity. He may talk sweet, but he felt dangerous.

Inching his chair closer to Athena, Giorgios placed his arm across her back and tried to engage her in conversation. Apparently, he didn't realize how much she knew about him and continued as if he were a welcomed member of the party.

Giorgios kept the champagne flowing with a heavy-hand, so she sipped her glass, but refused refills. Forty-five minutes passed before Athena could excuse herself again. She walked across the dance floor and out to the club's balcony. She needed time to think.

Her friend thought Giorgios was a beloved cousin, when in reality he had accused her future husband of theft. Athena should tell Heather who Giorgios really was. He had embezzled company funds, and had lied to save his own sleazy hide from Alexandros' wrath. Why was the serpent here now? Did he want to infuriate his cousins further, or was this some type of payback?

"Athena, is something wrong?" Heather joined her on the patio, obviously aware that all was not fine.

"No, it's nothing. I guess I'm a bit more tired than I initially thought. I just came out for some fresh air."

She could not put a damper on the evening. She would try to keep her friend away from Giorgios, minimizing contact until it was time to go home.

Grabbing Heather's hand, she guided her friend to the dance floor, hoping to put distance between them and Giorgios. Maria joined them for the next song, leaving brother and sister at the table.

The club was very crowded, and the friends danced amongst the tourists for a good while. Traditional Greek music began, and the women joined the long circles winding around the whole dance floor. When they passed their table, Eleni joined them, but Giorgios went to sit with some friends at the bar.

Returning to the table, Eleni raised her glass to the other women. "I want to make a toast. To Costa, the man who has brought us Heather, a friend we can grow old with!"

"*Gia mas!*"

The women clinked their glasses. Giorgio's dark gaze stretched across the club, locking on Athena as she brought the glass to her lips. She finished her glass and saw him stand, shaking his friend's hand. He walked towards the exit and she finally relaxed.

Everything would be okay, she reasoned. Giorgios had left, and she would not ruin Heather's party. Settling into her chair, she leaned comfortably on the table with her elbows.

"No, no special man in my life right now. I better put on my sneakers to catch that bouquet for luck then," Eleni said, pretending to lace her shoes and push up her sleeves. The women laughed and raised their glasses for a toast again.

Athena's fatigue rapidly increased and the loud music was starting to annoy her. Heather and the others went to dance, but Athena sat at the table feeling every bit of energy drain from her body. Ordering some mineral water, she hoped her head would feel better soon. The heat and noise of the club were making her dizzy. She'd wait for the water and then go out on the balcony for some more fresh air.

Alexandros stormed into Asteri. He scanned the room finding three of the women on the dance floor. Athena was not there. Fear ripped through him.

A few long strides and he saw her at the far side of the club at the champagne tables, Giorgios's arm wrapped around her. Her head rested on his cousin's shoulder, her eyes shut. Giorgios caressed the side of Athena's exposed neck as his mouth lowered to the smooth skin above her chest.

Alexandros did not think. He lurched forward, quickening his steps. Barely breathing, he closed the distance before his brother and the rest of the bachelor party even entered the room. His fingers wrapped around his cousin's collar pulling him out of his seat.

Maintaining a tight hold on Giorgio's shirt, Alexandros nudged Athena back down onto the chair.

Turning his attention back to his cousin, his eyes burned and he cursed in Greek.

"Don't touch what is mine," Alexandros growled, bringing his fist to split Giorgio's lip.

Costa pulled him off before he could get another punch in. "Alexandros, don't do this now. I'll handle it."

"It's already handled," Alexandros spat as his fingers tightened around Athena's arm and pulled her possessively against him. "Make sure he never walks on my side of the street again."

"He is not in rehab," Costa stated. "The authorities are on their way to take him in." He then gestured to Athena. "She doesn't look good. Should we call a doctor?"

Alexandros looked down and saw Athena's eyes flutter closed again. He loosened his grip and she slouched. Damn, she couldn't even stand.

"Next time there will be no authorities, just the priest and the grave diggers!" Alexandros warned Giorgio. He glared at his bloodied cousin as he gathered her limp body into his arms and carried Athena out to the car.

Keeping her on his lap as the driver closed the door, he cradled her against his body.

"What happened?" she whispered, her hand coming to rest on his heaving chest.

"Nothing, *agape mou,* nothing." Alexandros ran his fingers through her hair. "Sleep. I have you now," he said, kissing her head and pressing her closer to his heart.

Athena felt like home to him. She was a perfect fit. She was his unwinding. When he was with her, when he touched her, he felt complete. How could he have left her exposed like that?

He vowed that from that moment forward, he would not allow anything to hurt her again.

Chapter Twelve

Alexandros opened his eyes as the first morning rays of light danced into the bedroom. He pulled Athena a little bit closer. Her hair sprawled across his chest and her soft breath caressed his skin. She slept soundly, safe in his arms, making a small noise with each breath escaping her lips.

He gently traced the outline of her neck as she dozed. His fingertips relished the journey on the smooth golden surface of her skin and ached to explore further. Painfully aware of her warmth settling against his abdomen, her leg cradling his thigh, and her female scent in his nostrils, all setting his loins aflame, he shifted away from her.

If circumstances were different, he would be waking her at this moment, making real the images of heated lovemaking that tortured him as he watched her sleep.

He pictured her opening her eyes as he entered her soft and sweet body. He would kiss the morning sleep from her mouth, taste those rising nipples that taunted him through the white undershirt he had dressed her in, and make her undeniably his. He wanted her to awaken just as he possessed her, for her eyes to fill with desire for him. Her pupils would grow wide, her breathing would be fierce, and her fingers would bury themselves in his back.

Enough!

This was absurd. She needed him as much as he did her. He would not fantasize about her any further. She must realize, as soon as possible, that her rule was not meant for him.

He was the exception.

Brushing his lips over hers, he removed her golden arm from his chest and slowly stepped out of bed.

Alexandros turned on the shower and let the cold water soothe his skin. Hitting the wall with his fist, he let some explicit Greek words escape his lips.

He should have anticipated last night. He should have remained in Athens until Giorgios was locked behind bars. Athena had paid the price for his lack of foresight, and he did not want to think about what could have happened if he had not found her when he did.

When the water turned from cold to frigid, Alexandros decided to end the shower. Knotting a towel around his middle, he took out a bottle of water from the room's fridge and went to sit beside Athena on the bed. He stroked her cheek until her eyes opened to his.

"*Kalimera, agape mou.*"

Pulling the sheet up around her, she moved away. He watched realization dawn in Athena's eyes as she noticed that she was in his undershirt and that he was on her bed in a towel. Her eyes asked him what her mouth could not.

"Don't worry. You would remember if I had made love to you last night," he assured her.

"What happened? Why are you here?" she asked, sitting up and rubbing her forehead with stiff fingers.

"He drugged you," Alexandros said, fighting to maintain his control. Pushing the water into her hands, he motioned for her to drink as he explained. "*Bastardos*! I should have known he would come after you, I should've been with you."

"Please, Alexandros, I don't understand. Tell me again what happened."

He raked his fingers through his hair. "Last night, Giorgios came into Asteri looking to take something from me. He wanted to find my Achilles heel and strike. He knew of you because I'd stupidly told him about you when I'd returned form Naples. Being a fool, I confided in him. That was before I knew what he was doing. Giorgios knew how I feel about you and figured he would get to me through you."

Athena nodded, indicating that he should continue.

"Eleni told him about the bachelorette party she planned, and luckily, she told me too. I asked my friend Takis, the club's manager, to watch out for you. Thank God I did that at least."

"But how did I— did we, get here?"

"*Thee mou*! Do you not see?" Smacking his thighs, he stood, shook his head, and paced around the bed. "Takis thought he saw Giorgio drop something in one of the drinks, your drink. He realized that after you returned from dancing, before Giorgio went to sit by the bar, you never got up from your seat. He called me."

"Heather?"

"Eleni and Heather had no clue what he did to you, so when you said you wanted to rest, the others went ahead to the dance floor. I found you in his arms."

"*Thee mou!*" she cried. Scalding tears rolled down her cheeks. The site of them burned a hole in his heart.

"No, not tears, I cannot see you cry." Alexandros sat beside her and wiped her cheeks with his thumbs. "Takis was watching. He was ready to intervene if I did not make it in time, or if Giorgio tried to remove you from the club. *Thee mou*, I did make it."

"With some questions, we found out what Giorgio had purchased from an unsavory character earlier last night." He took her tight fist into his hand and held it close. "The doctor said it would not be harmful to you and that you could just sleep it off. It simply made you unaware of what was happening, and you could not think for yourself. Doctor Petrakis assured me there are no lasting effects."

"Where are my clothes?"

"I brought you home, helped you change, and you slept. Thankfully, safe at home."

"Just slept?" she asked, her voice trembling.

"Just slept," he assured her. "Drink some more water. It will help your head."

She gathered her knees to her chest, rocking her body as she drank. The pillow beside her had been used, and both sides of the bed were rumpled. She had shared his bed and did not even remember it. Her gaze darted around the room and found their clothes spread on the window seat.

"Are you hurt?" Athena couldn't see anything, but the clothes were soiled.

"No. Why?"

She pointed to his shirt. "There is blood on your sleeve."

"That is his blood. Not mine, his. *Bastardos!*"

She continued to rock on the bed as he paced the room.

"I'm sorry, *agape mou*. I should have protected you better. I should have anticipated last night. It is my fault he had the opportunity to do this horrible thing to you. Athena, please forgive me."

Athena watched his shoulders come closer together as he sat on the chair and massaged his temples. She felt his regret, his misplaced sense of failure. Last night she'd recognized that Giorgio was up to no good, but she had refused to do anything about it. It wasn't Alexandros' fault, how could he have known?

She got out of bed, walked to him and tilted his face up to hers. "I needed you, and you came."

Wrapping his arms around her knees, Alexandros pulled her toward him. He kissed her stomach and then stood to take her face in his palms.

"I could never forgive myself if anything happened to you. Thank God you are okay."

"It's my fault." She looked up into his hurt eyes. "When I saw Giorgios, I knew that he wasn't right. I was aware of what happened between you, but I don't think the other women were. My instinct told me to leave the club, but I didn't want to ruin the night. I didn't want to put a damper on the party. I made the wrong choice. I should've listened to my gut."

"It is definitely not your fault. Don't ever say that. But, *I* promise not to leave you accessible to anything like that again. I promise to listen to *my instinct,* and I will be with you. Do not worry about Giorgios anymore. He has been dealt with. He is in custody. I won't let him near you again."

Feeling her knees wobble, she sat in the chair. Alexandros tried to make her comfortable, but she wanted time alone. He told her to go back to bed, take the aspirin he had left on the nightstand, and rest. He went to get something for breakfast.

Athena could not stay in bed. She got up, determined to put last night behind her and make the most of the day. Putting his shirt in the sink to soak, she made the bed and opened all the shutters to air out the room.

Something deep inside was different. She shrugged, deciding not to analyze any further.

Upon Alexandros' return, she was showered, dressed, and sitting on the veranda by the little blue table.

He laid the tray down and looked at her with worried eyes. "Do you feel better now?"

"I do, and I'll be good as new after I have some coffee and a newspaper."

They ate in silence, reading the papers. She was so grateful for his comforting company and allowed herself to relax.

He folded the NEA and appeared to be examining her with a long, detailed sweep of his gaze over her body. "Do you really feel all right?"

"I really do." She flashed him what she hoped was an assuring smile.

"How can you answer with the easy smile of someone who has spent the last week relaxing on the beach? There is no trace of the night's happenings on your gorgeous face." He grinned approvingly and kissed the back of her hand. "I'm awed with your resilience."

"Stop it." She shifted her balance. "It's not that—"

"Athena, you're a very strong person, and I admire you more with every moment we spend together."

"Sure. So amazing that I put myself in danger last night."

"Don't talk like that. It wasn't your fault."

"Forget it." She waived her hand in the air. "I don't want to discuss it any more. Let's do something special today. Okay?"

"What do you want to do?"

"Anything." She shrugged and tucked her fingers under her thighs. "What did you have planned?"

"I wanted to pickup a wedding gift for Heather. The store is in Athens, so I was thinking of combining the shopping trip with a visit to one of our ships. Do you feel up for a helicopter ride today, or would you rather I have the present brought here?"

"Do you know what you want to get?"

"Not specifically, but I know where I want to buy it and approximately what I want. They could send a few pieces, and I will choose. The other option is that we go together and make a day of it. We could spend the afternoon shopping and watch Athens light up after the sun goes down. I would really enjoy spending time together, if you feel up to it."

"I absolutely adore Athens at night." Athena's spirits lifted as she anticipated the trip. "My favorite thing to do is to sit at Lycavitos Mount and look down at the city when it is dark. I just don't want Heather to think I abandoned her."

"What if we return to Santorini for after a late dinner, and we bring back Athens's best *galaktoboureko* for dessert?"

"It sounds fantastic. *Pame,* let's go."

Alexandros stood and walked behind her chair. His long arms covered hers and he entwined their fingers as he softly kissed the side of her neck.

"I will make a few calls while you get ready, *agape mou.*"

This time she enjoyed hearing him call her his love. Something had changed in her, in her feelings for him. She smiled and kissed his hand as it lingered near her shoulders. He slowly let go and walked away to make the arrangements.

Chapter Thirteen

Athena strolled into her room and went straight for the wardrobe closet. She swung open the heavy wooden door and spent a few seconds surveying her clothes. It was too warm for slacks and shorts were inappropriate for the trip, so she turned her attention to the neatly arranged dresses. After a few minutes of flipping through the hanging garments, she decided on a cream-colored linen sheath dress. She added a pair of designer sandals and a matching clutch to complete the simple outfit.

Looking into the mirror, she was satisfied with the way the dress complimented her figure. Her hair fell loose down her back and the sun had bronzed her cheeks. She added a small amount of mascara and lip-gloss to complete her look.

She was looking forward to spending the day with Alexandros in Athens. She could hardly wait to survey the tempting shops with their unique pieces not found in any department store, and of course, the most enjoyable part of shopping in Athens was the level of service the storeowners there offered to each of their patrons. They always seemed to take a personal interest in accommodating their client's needs.

But most of all, she wanted to be with Alexandros. To sit beside him and feel his thigh brush hers, to walk with him as his arm wrapped around her waist, bringing her into contact with his body. Somehow, she had stopped thinking of him as a Greek playboy. He was Alexandros, a man she wanted to know better.

She wanted to experience what lovers of the past three thousand years had, to look into his eyes and lose herself in the taste of his mouth below the awe of the ancient Acropolis, the birthplace of the modern civilized world. There was nothing civilized about her thoughts, though. She yearned to abandon all logic, to be and to feel nothing but the joy of being his.

The soft knock at the door sobered her mind.

"One moment, I'm still getting ready."

"It's just me," replied Heather as she opened the door and stepped into the room. "Getting ready for what?"

"*Kalimera.* Alexandros and I are going to Athens for a few hours."

"Are you feeling alright? I was worried about you after Costa explained what had happened. I wanted to come and make sure you would be okay, but Costa insisted that Alexandros was taking good care of you." Heather gave Athena a quick hug before she sat on the edge of the bed. "You know, that gorgeous brother-in-law of mine stormed into Asteri, punched Giorgios, pulled you into his arms and carried you away."

"He carried me out of the club?"

"Yeah, it was like a scene out of one of those romance novels or something. I think he was breathing fire holding you so tight, keeping you safe from all the bad in the world, specifically from Giorgios."

Heather went quiet and looked at her feet. "I'm so sorry Athena. I had no idea who Giorgios was. You did though, and that is why you were so edgy. You should have told me and we could have left."

"I know, but I didn't want to ruin the evening for you. I thought I could handle him, and then I thought he had left." Athena said remorsefully.

"Well we're very lucky Alexandros thought ahead and let Takis know we were going to be there. I had no clue Giorgios was all over you until the guys came storming in. The place went silent, except for the music, and Alexandros made it known that you were with him and no one had any right to touch you."

"How did he do that?"

"Simple. He said it. Alexandros is a very, very respected man, and I do not think anyone would question him. Besides, he looked very intimidating stalking across the floor and punching out his cousin. Carrying you out of there eliminated any doubt that you were his. I knew you were safe with him."

Athena sat beside her friend and stared in disbelief.

"You should have seen him," Heather continued. "Well you did, but you obviously don't remember. There is no question as to how he feels about you, or what he would do for you."

Unable to speak, Athena tried to digest the scene in her mind.

"You know how he is with his family?" Heather asked, and Athena nodded remembering the afternoon on the veranda and the phone call. "He is very protective of the people he loves, and you are obviously one of those people. He must really love you. I think he would do anything for you."

"Heather, you're too much of a romantic. Maybe something was slipped into your drink too, and you hallucinated all of this." Athena was trying to lighten the mood, but could see that her friend was not buying it. "He is being nice and attentive to me because of you and Costa. We're just friends."

Heather raised an inquisitive blonde eyebrow and her lips curved into a smile. Her eyes sparkled as Athena continued to deny what was happening before them.

"Okay, perhaps a little more than friends. Alexandros is not what I expected him to be. He's really nice."

"Nice? Perhaps that drink did something to *your* brain. He is amazing, and he is crazy about you. Costa says he has never seen his brother show any feelings toward a woman in front of the family before, and Alexandros is definitely not hiding his feelings for you."

"You're exaggerating. We may like spending time together, but we only have a week. Nothing happens in a week. After the wedding, we will go back to our separate lives, very far away from each other. We live and work on different sides of the globe, and we have very different ideas on love and romance."

"Is that so? What do you mean by different?" Heather said and started to giggle.

"Come on, Heather, stop teasing me. You know how I feel about Greek playboys. I can never be involved with one. I can't take the chance."

"What about my Costa? Why was he worth taking the chance?"

"Costa is different. He was a real friend."

"That's right. You gave Costa a chance, and he became your friend. He is Greek and by many people's considerations a playboy. Others see him as a perfect catch. For you he is a great friend, but for me he is the man I want to share the rest of my life with. Do you think I would ever have known that if I was as closed-minded as you?"

"Come on, Heather, we are discussing apples and oranges. Besides, both, you and Costa, were willing participants in your relationship. You were both ready to commit exclusively to one another. You are meant for each other." Athena knew she was rambling, grasping at straws to avoid the truth.

Heather merely smiled. "Listen, just go have a good time and keep your mind open. Let your heart guide you, and perhaps you'll be surprised. It is so obvious to everyone but you. Baba says that was how Mama was when he first met her."

"You've discussed this with your in-laws?" Athena rubbed her neck within an inch of scarring it with burn marks. "Heather, how could you do that?"

"*I* have not said a word. They are the ones who think it is so natural to discuss their son's love life. To be honest with you, I agree with them."

Athena stared blankly at her best friend. She and Alexandros were a topic of discussion for his parents. How could she possibly face them and share in her best friend's life if they thought she had had a week's tryst with their oldest son? Athena would lose respect in their eyes. How could they share a Christmas, perhaps the births of Heather's children, the christenings, and a casual Easter barbecue?

"All right, forget what I think." Heather raised her hand and smoothed the worry lines above Athena's brow. Standing from the bed and bending to kiss Athena's cheek, she added some soft and reassuring words. "Just be a little more open-minded and let nature take its course. I'm sure Alexandros will make you see the truth."

"And the truth is *he* has no interest in a long-term relationship." Hands fisted tight against her thighs, Athena took an offensive stance. "*He* is very happy with his single status, and *we* are simply going to have a good time without letting it all get too physical."

"Are you ready to go, *agape mou*? Athens is waiting for us. *Ante, koukla mou*." Alexandros called from downstairs and interrupted Athena's explanation. His masculine voice sent goose bumps to Athena's flesh.

Heather giggled. "Yeah sure, *koukla mou*, his doll*, agape mou*, his love. You've really convinced me now," she said, using her fingers to make the little quotation marks. "Lets go, Athens is waiting for *us*, goose bump lady."

"Got to go, darling. See you later." Athena smiled and smacked her friend's shoulder. "*We* will bring *galaktoboureko* for dessert tonight."

"Tonight? Maybe you two will *be* dessert and not come back till the morning?" Heather whispered as the pair walked towards the stairs landing.

"Not too physical, remember? Thanks to you, I need to face the family after this week is over." Caution flared in Athena's eyes.

"You mean *if* this is over in a week."

Heather kissed her friend goodbye and skipped down the stairs to Alexandros, kissing him as well.

"*Gia sas*! Have fun, and don't do anything I wouldn't do." Heather waved over her shoulder and walked away.

"What is that all about?" Alexandros asked, placing his hand on the small of Athena's back and leading her toward the helicopter pad.

"Nothing much. She has pre-wedding giggles and all that."

"I'm glad she's happy. My brother is very blessed to have her. I like her so much more every time I see her. She is a Strintzaris already."

Looking into his eyes, Athena caught a glimmer of something that was not there before, a combination of warmth, possession and belonging. He turned toward the helicopter and guided her to lower her head and get closer. She must have imagined what she saw, a likely side effect of Heather's giddy musings.

Chapter Fourteen

Leaning across her body, Alexandros tugged at Athena's safety belt. His proximity and masculine presence immediately made her nipples harden. Completing the belt check, he sat back and his upper arm brushed against her heaving chest. The contact caused a ripple of sensation to race through her body and a small moan to escape her lips.

"You're not nervous to fly, are you?" His gaze locked on hers, and she thought she'd go cross-eyed watching his lips touch her nose. He then took her hand in his and held it reassuringly.

She shook her head side to side, but held tight to his hand anyway. His fingers stroked her knuckles, and she decided to let things take their course as Heather had suggested. She smiled at him, and he leaned in to give her a soft, but sensual kiss.

The blades accelerated and the helicopter lifted from the ground. He intensified the kiss, letting his tongue trail her needy lips. She was consumed by the desire to taste him as his other hand came in front and cupped her face.

"I look forward to spending the day with you." He spoke softly as he stroked her cheek. "We need time to ourselves, away from the family, away from all the wedding preparations, and away from Santorini."

"Speaking of which, Santorini is very beautiful from the air. The colors of the sea, the cliffs, and the beaches are amazing. The volcano in the middle looks like it is standing guard over the harbor." She gazed out the window, amazed at the natural beauty that emanated such power and awe.

"Tomorrow we can sail to the volcano if you would like. Have you ever walked on a live volcano?"

"We could do that?" She sat at attention, shaking her leg up and down in a quick rhythm. Squeezing his hand, she nodded enthusiastically and said, "I'd like it very much. Maybe we'll catch a glimpse of the lost land of Atlantis on the way. You know, that's what we learned in school. Atlantis is buried in the waters around Santorini."

"They've found ruins of a city below the water. If you want, we can do some diving as well. It's really a sight to see. The first time I saw the sun reflect off the columns, the fish swim around them...I cannot describe it. You need to see it for yourself."

She hesitated. "I've never been scuba diving. Can we see the ruins if we snorkel?"

"On a calm sea, we can. However, it's better if we go under." His cell phone rang and he quickly pulled it from his pocket to check the number. "I'm sorry, *agape mou*. I need to take this."

She nodded and smiled, letting him pull her close, and settling against him for the rest of the ride.

They sat close, arms and fingers entwined, and Athena allowed herself to thoroughly enjoy the scenic flight over the Greek islands. It was a magical flight, the sheer majesty of the rocky islands rising from the azure waters of the Mediterranean, nearly took her breath away. She was further enthralled by a group of spotted dolphins playing in a ferry's wake.

Approximately twenty minutes into the ride, Alexandros finished his business call. He asked the pilot to slow and hover over the canal between the mainland and the former southern part of the mainland, Peloponnesus.

"Look, there's a cruise ship crossing the Isthmus of Corinthos." Alexandros pointed to the precise cut in the land. "The ship is pretty large and probably had to time the crossing with high tide. The yellow bumpers are barely clearing the sides."

"Wow, it's amazing how the little tug boat can pull that big ship." Indicating the tiny boat, Athena looked to Alexandros for more explanations.

"Yes. Those tugs are great. When we come into port in shallow harbors, or it is difficult to maneuver within, we always use the tugs to pull us into the harbor, and then later, back out to sea. You'll see the Argyris III within a few minutes. It's docked and unloading in Elefsina."

"I'll have a few words with the captain, then give you a quick tour." Alexandros gathered his briefcase as he spoke. "I'd like to get to Athens before two o'clock so that we can pick up the gift and have the rest of the day to ourselves."

They watched the rugged coast of the mainland as the helicopter made its way over the emerald blue sea toward the Argyris III. Elefsina had been a commercial port for over three thousand years, and the neighboring towns produced some of the best naval officers in the world. Now, various freighters and tankers dotted the waters, attesting to the port's continued importance.

Argyris III came into view, and the helicopter landed on the port's helipad.

Embarking onto the ship, Athena wondered in awe over its enormity. Huge cranes at the front unloaded boxes like huge presents onto the dock. Alexandros explained that the ship was a general cargo vessel returning from Japan, and was transporting automobiles in the containers on deck. Various types of electrical goods were contained in the hull.

Unfortunately, the ship had encountered rough seas on the voyage. He wanted to inspect the damage himself before Argyris III headed to Skaramangas Shipyards, near Athens, for general inspection and repairs.

The ship's officers lined up to receive them.

"Welcome aboard," said a very handsome, fifty-something Captain Karavokiris. He extended his hand to Alexandros. "We're very pleased that you were able to make it, Mr. Strintzaris. Allow us to offer you and your guest some refreshments."

The captain led the couple below the bridge and down two narrow flights of stairs into the Officers' Dining Room. A simple assortment of snacks and drinks filled a long table. Alexandros sat at the head of a clothed table and Athena was placed to his right. The captain sat on Alexandros' left, and introductions were made for her benefit. After drinks were served, Captain Karavokiris requested his briefcase be brought to the table.

The Captain reviewed the ship's timeline with Alexandros and reassured him that Argyris III would be back in dock four days before her next scheduled voyage. Alexandros concentrated on the reports of damage the ship had sustained.

"Miss Lakis, perhaps you would like to join us and tour Argyris III at the same time?" the captain suggested when Alexandros finished examining the reports.

She nodded, and they set out for a visual inspection of the physical damage.

Athena followed the men up to the bridge. The captain continued to inform Alexandros of the ship's status as they entered.

"As you were able to ascertain from the reports, the *pilotirio*, the bridge, shows no evidence of a difficult crossing. All the navigational equipment is intact. The monitoring gauges show no mechanical or engine damage. The only damage that we are currently aware of is on the port side. The railings and the hinges that support the lifeboats will need to be repaired, as well as two of the portholes on deck four. I am proud to say that she is a strong ship, and no one would guess what she has been through the past two weeks."

"*Bravo*, very nice to hear," Alexandros said. "Honestly, Captain, I expect nothing less of her when she has someone like you at the helm. It is a reflection of your ability and great competence that the ship runs as well as she does. I'll be in contact with you as she enters Skaramangas and again as she is ready to depart. We've taken enough of your valuable time for now. I will tour the remaining damage on my own. Thank you."

"As you wish, sir. It's a pleasure and an honor to captain one of your vessels, Mr. Strintzaris. I'll be sure to present all the repair reports to you myself, if you will be available, when they are complete?"

"I will. Thank you, again." Alexandros shook the man's hand and turned to Athena. "I think we can manage the rest on our own."

"Thank you for your gracious hospitality. It was a pleasure meeting you," Athena said, accepting the captain's hand.

"The pleasure was mine, *Kyria*." The captain lifted her hand to his lips.

That was a first. Nobody had called her 'kyria' before.

"*Kyria?* Why not miss or *despinis*?" she asked Alexandros as they walked on the deck, inspecting the damaged railings.

"Because, he is a smart man, and he knows you're not an available *despinis*." Taking her hand in his, he smiled at her as they descended the stairs. "Stop analyzing every little word, *koukla mou*. It's the book that you need to concern yourself with."

"What's that supposed to mean?"

"It means we are each authors of our own books or artists of our own frescoes. Concern yourself with the emotions the painting on the wall invokes, not just a single brush stroke." He shrugged his shoulders in a typically Greek way and flashed a wicked smile.

She couldn't help but return the gesture, and formed her lips into a playful smirk. "I didn't know you had such a poetic way of expressing your thoughts."

Alexandros released her hand and pressed his lips against her ear, a glimmer of mischief playing in his eyes as he kept her waiting for a response.

"There are many things about me you don't know, and you need to learn," he whispered, entwining his fingers in her hair and bringing his mouth down on hers. His heated lips applied pressure, his tongue skimmed over her teeth, and then he delved deliciously deeper. A small moan escaped her.

"Oh?"

"Unfortunately, this isn't the right place or time to acquire that knowledge." Pulling away, he laughed lightly. "Come on, *koukla,* we need to stop on deck four for the damaged portholes, and then we'll finish above deck so we can go."

Recapturing her hand, he turned and led her down the stairs. He didn't let go until they were back in the helicopter and he needed to secure their safety belts.

They were over Athens before noon. At first, Athena sat quietly enjoying the view of the ancient city that held a very special place in her heart, and then she began to share her thoughts with Alexandros.

"When we arrived for summer holidays with my family, we always spent the first two or three days in Athens. While we were younger, Mom and Dad did the tourist things with us. We'd start with the changing of the guard at the Syntagma."

Alexandros pointed to the Parliament building, the Syntagma, on their left as she spoke.

"My brothers and I liked to have ice cream at the Zapeion in the National Gardens next. We'd linger there for the afternoon in the shade of those massive trees and search the grounds for archeological treasures. We'd end the afternoons at the modern Olympic Stadium for a jog around the track. Usually jetlag would win by then and we'd go back to the hotel.

"The second day we were up hours before our parents and were ready to trek up to the Acropolis. We'd spend the morning asking thousands of questions about the construction of the Parthenon and the amazing ability to haul all that marble to the top without the help of modern technology. The same questions each year. By the afternoon, my parents were grateful for us to sit at Thanassi's Kebabs and fill our mouths so that they could enjoy the peace for a half hour. We had the same routine for ten years or so. I'm surprised they humored us like that each year, but they did."

Alexandros enjoyed listening to her speak about her childhood and her family. She'd met his family, but he didn't know hers. Families such as Athena's were very tightly knit. Spending years secluded and away from extended family, they found support and love from deep within the home. He wanted to know more about her, which meant knowing more about her family.

"So when did your parents stop humoring you?" Alexandros asked, prompting her to tell him more.

"They didn't. We still do the first afternoon thing, when we all travel together that is. Only, as we got older, we began to win over the jetlag on the first night. Well, except for Tony. He still enjoys his sleep that first night. He loves his sleep."

Her face, bright with the recollection, animated her love for her brothers. Her hands spoke volumes of emotion and the small crinkle her nose made when she emphasized Tony's need for sleep, squeezed at his heart.

Such a passionate woman, no way am I letting her go.

"Demo and I started going out to the cafes and later to the *tavernas* until all hours of the night. We were usually too tired for the Acropolis in the morning, so we used to meet them at Thanassi's for lunch. We joked that the Acropolis has been there for three thousand years and it would be there until the next year. Every couple of years, we got everybody to wait for us until the afternoon though. We could never turn our backs on the Acropolis, regardless of how old we got or how long the nights became." She raised her shoulders in a casual shrug and smiled with the memories.

"Your family sounds fantastic. I would like to meet them," he said sincerely. "It seems like you will be showing me my own city today. How about lunch at Thanassi's then?"

"Yes," she said, and smiled. "I was hoping for that. A visit to Athens without one of their kebabs would not seem right."

"It would be my pleasure to make things right for you, *agape mou*."

The helicopter landed atop the Strintzaris building in the heart of the city. Alexandros walked her through the company headquarters and introduced her to some of his valued employees. They were in his office suite looking across the National Gardens when Costa called.

Alexandros took the call at his desk, assuring his brother Athena was fine. He explained that they would do some shopping and enjoy the city for the day, but they'd be back on the island for a late dinner. He then requested details of what was happening with Giorgios and was happy with the information he received.

The conversation turned to business and he watched Athena relax on the couch in front of the floor length window. She slipped off her shoes and pulled her feet under her. Her eyes drifted closed and she leaned her head on the arm of the couch. Within moments, she was asleep.

Alexandros bent and kissed the tip of her nose. He admired her strength and her fortitude considering the previous night's horrendous events. She looked so peaceful and beautiful. He contemplated moving her into the adjacent bedroom he used when he was unable to leave the office, but after watching her for a few minutes, he decided to let her sleep where she was. If he woke her, she might not agree to take the extra time to rest. He pulled the curtains to darken the room and covered her with a soft cashmere throw from the bedroom.

Sitting back at his desk, he called his personal assistant and requested some files, instructing her not to knock and to enter cautiously. He then silenced the ringers on the phones and turned toward the computer to work.

Chapter Fifteen

She woke to a ringing telephone. Sitting up, she looked around the dark office and saw the only light was coming from a door slightly ajar on the far end. She was alone.

The phone continued to ring.

Bringing her feet to the floor, she traced the ringing to her handbag. She reached across the coffee table and pulled out her personal cellular.

"*Ne?*"

"Hello, *koukla.* Don't tell me I woke you?"

"Demo! *Gia sou*! It's good to hear from you. You sound like you're next door or something."

"That depends on where you are, *koukla.*"

"I'm in Athens. Where are you?"

"What a coincidence. So am I." Her brother was teasing her. He wasn't supposed to be in Greece for another ten days. She was collecting her thoughts when he spoke again. "Athena, you still awake?"

"Yes, Demo. I'm sorry. I just woke from a nap, and I'm a little disoriented. How are you?"

"Napping in the middle of the day? That's Tony's job, not yours." He chuckled. "And I'm just fine, thank you for asking. Winding down from the flight."

"You really are in Athens? Really?"

"Really. I called for you in Santorini and Heather told me you were here. Too bad I've already arranged to leave for Crete tonight. I'm on the ten o'clock ferry to Chania. I didn't know I'd have company if I stayed in Athens. Will I see you before I leave?"

"Yes, I think so. I need to check with Alexandros and make sure the time works out. Where are you and how can I reach you?"

"Back up a minute, *koukla*. Alexandros who?"

Athena cringed. Alexandros' name had rolled off her lips too easily. She tried to brush it off, but her brother's reaction had her on edge.

"Come on, Demo, stop playing with me. Alexandros is Heather's soon to be brother in-law. We came up to Athens to do some shopping and run a few errands. Now give me your number."

"And you happen to be sleeping in the middle of the day while running errands with Alexandros Strintzaris?"

She knew Demo wanted her to elaborate, but she wasn't going to do so. She was a grown woman now, and she didn't have to answer to him.

"Cut it out, and stop acting like such a big brother. Give me the number, and I'll call you back in a few minutes."

"Don't forget, I *am* your big brother," he laughed. "Will I meet this Alexandros if I give you my number?

"Perhaps."

Athena jotted down the phone number and sent her brother a kiss over the phone line before disconnecting. Walking toward the door, she saw Alexandros at a conference table with some of his executives. She caught his eye, and he smiled at her.

Quickly excusing himself, he stood and walked away from the table. He stepped through the office and closed the door behind him as he turned on a light switch.

"You look far too tempting when you wake up." He wrapped his arms around her waist and pulled her against him. Feeling her against him was so right. He smiled. "Give me a minute to get rid of the suits in the other room. I'll be right back."

"Alexandros, wait one moment." Her voice prevented his feet from moving. "Can we talk first?"

"Of course. Is everything okay?"

"Absolutely, actually more than okay." There was a twinkle in her eyes. "My brother just called and he is in Athens. I was wondering if we had time to meet him for a drink or something?"

"We will make time." Alexandros relaxed and pulled her close, kissing the top of her head. "I got worried you were not feeling well. You slept for over three hours. Which brother and where is he so that we can send a car?"

"It's Demosthenis. I promised to call him back with the details since we still have to go for Heather's gift."

"The gift is taken care of, unless you don't think she will like it. I put it in the bedroom on the nightstand. Take a look and give me your opinion. You can freshen up in there while I wrap up the meeting, and then we'll go to Thanassi's for lunch. *Entaxi, agape mou?"*

"Okay. Thank you for letting me rest. I needed it more than I thought. I feel much better now."

"I don't know how you managed to get up and function so early this morning. You amaze me." He ran his palm across her cheek and laid his thumb on her full lips. He applied soft pressure and her lips gently parted as he bent to seal them with a kiss. She responded and fell further into his embrace.

Tasting her sweetness, he acknowledged to himself that only the arrival of her brother was helping him control the physical need to possess her completely. He ran his hands down her back and rested them on her curved bottom. His thighs felt at home between hers, but he knew he must curtail the intimate contact immediately if he was to maintain control.

"Go, *agape mou,* freshen up and I will be ready shortly." He breathed with great restraint as he guided her towards the bedroom door. "Plan the remainder of the day as you would like. I'm in complete agreement."

He had left the decision up to her. He knew they were growing together, he felt the intimacy building between them with each passing hour. She would find a way to show him when she was ready. He made every conscious effort not to rush her physically and to allow her the time to accept him, body and soul.

Entering the bedroom, Athena considered her options. She could plan to stay here for a while longer. She wanted to be alone with Alexandros, she wanted to love him and let him love her. She could linger in the bath and invite him to join her when he came back. Her thoughts raced to foggy mirrors, tousled bed sheets, and excruciating physical pleasure. Her stomach tightened into a knot and she hesitated to proceed. Choosing the second option of readying herself to spend time with him out on the busy city streets, before meeting with her brother, was less complicated.

Her brother!

She dialed Demo's number and arranged to meet at the Zapeion café. Refusing a car, he assured her he was looking forward to seeing his little sister and her new friend. Demo tried to press her for more information on her relationship with Alexandros, but she refused to take the bait. They said their goodbyes, and she turned to see three pretty packages on the bed. She walked over to them, picked up the rose across the top of the two larger ones and read a note that told her they were for her.

The first box contained bath products from one of Athens' most exclusive body shops. It was a complete assortment of shampoos, shower gels, creams and even a toothbrush.

She carried the box into the en-suite bathroom and noted the reason for the gift. All the products in the cabinets and on the shelves were positively masculine; the scent of Alexandros' cologne filled the room. Not that she would have minded immersing her body in his scent, but she found the gift to be extremely thoughtful and welcoming.

Taking extra care to unwrap the ribbon on the second box, she found a beautiful silk halter dress. It was a warm ivory shade with a bold gold flower print along the empire waist. It stopped just above the knee and highlighted her shapely long legs as well as her smooth shoulders and full breasts.

She found delicate lace undergarments beneath the dress and smiled at the thought of having Alexandros remove them from her body. She decided to wait a while longer for such a pleasure. Athena peeked in on the third box on the nightstand, Heather's gift. It was gorgeous. No one could ever accuse Alexandros of having bad taste.

She entered the main office dressed and ready for the afternoon in the city. Alexandros had changed out of his business suit into a pair of well-tailored black linen slacks and a fresh, cream-colored linen shirt. Despite the casual folded sleeves and the open collar, his appearance shouted power and strength. He caressed her body with his dark gaze as he ordered the car.

"Thank you," she said, turning to afford him a full view. The skirt billowed about her as she curtsied.

"My pleasure, pretty lady." He stepped beside her and offered the crook of his arm. "Where to?"

"Why Thanassi's, of course." She took his arm and they walked to the private lift in his office suite. She tapped her fingers on his forearm as they waited. "Demosthenis will meet us at Zapeion at six-thirty. Until then, we can roam the streets by the Monastiraki and enjoy the view of the Acropolis from below."

The driver left them a few blocks from the restaurant because the area was only for pedestrian traffic. Strolling arm in arm, they arrived at the busy sidewalk *taverna* to find a table set with roses waiting for them. A long line of hungry tourists and locals waited, but the owner bypassed the line and personally escorted Athena and Alexandros to their seats. A bottle of cold mineral water was opened, and they ordered the favorite Greek salad, French fries, and the infamous kebab platter.

Savoring the simple meal, they spent an hour enjoying the street musicians as they serenaded the patrons. Athena expressed her approval of the gorgeous necklace and bracelet Alexandros had picked for Heather. It was a LaLaounis design, with hand set beads of twenty-four carat gold and emeralds meant to replicate the jewelry worn by the aristocracy during the times of Alexander the Great.

It was a gift his new sister would surely treasure.

"I'm so glad you like it," he said. "I hope she doesn't think it is too traditional."

"No. It is perfect. She'll love it. It is absolutely gorgeous."

He filled her in on some business talk about the hospitality industry and relayed greetings from her boss.

"Do you remember when we first met in Naples, and I kidded with Luca about luring you to Strintzaris?"

She nodded.

"Well, what do you think? I would love to have you closer, and that could easily be accomplished if we worked together. You're very talented. We would be very lucky to have you as part of the team."

"It wouldn't be fair to Luca. He took the risk on me, and he'd lose the profit."

Furrowing his brows, he asked her to explain what she meant.

"I'm not supposed to discuss this, but I think I owe you an explanation." Taking a deep breath, she told him the whole story of her plans for the resort on Crete, all the while wondering if he would get up from the table and walk away from her for good.

Alexandros just listened with a stoic face that belonged on these ancient streets. When she was done, he met her gaze and surprised her with a stunning grin.

"*Bravo, koukla mou.* You are extremely resourceful," he said, pride the prominent emotion displayed on his handsome face. "A true Greek tycooness—if there is such a word."

Relief flooded through her. "You're funny," she added. "I'm sorry I couldn't be upfront from the start. It was a business decision, not a personal one. Demo has advised me not to let anyone know in case it should be leaked to the press, and the resort won't be able to benefit from the Giardetti name."

"I understand that completely." He nodded, running his fingers through his hair. "What I don't understand is why you didn't let your brothers finance the deal."

"I told you on the beach. Remember? I want to do it on my own merits. I don't want to ride their coattails."

"You are determined." He shook his head. "Well, you did it, and now there is no reason for it any more. I could settle the deal you have with Luca, and then you'd have Strintzaris resources at your disposal. I'll pay Luca the profit loss upfront."

"No, it would set my plans off if I had to pay interest on them in advance." Athena calculated numbers as she spoke and didn't understand the purpose of such a move.

"Personally, I would be very happy if you were here in Greece. I want to help you and be able to work together. If you desire, you could set the schedule to pay back Strintzaris. It isn't an issue."

Alexandros skimmed his thumb over her knuckles when it became clear to her. He was talking on a personal, not professional, level and her pride wouldn't allow such a deal. If she'd wanted to secure her goals in such a matter, she would have accepted her brothers' offer to back the deal. No, she needed to stay with the original plan.

"It isn't a good idea to mix business with pleasure." She looked away from his eyes. "Besides, I can't do that to Giardetti, I cannot abandon them and walk away. They're counting on me specifically for the Crete Hotel."

"Don't just walk away. Give Luca proper notice, we'll pay for any inconvenience, and then you'll be free. I want you to stay. We're professionals, and we can separate business and pleasure."

Knowing Greek men, she knew he didn't see any need to make that separation, but he would if it convinced her to stay. If she weren't familiar with the way Greek men thought, she would have been angry. However, she knew he didn't want to demean her abilities. He simply wanted to keep things 'in the family'—for lack of a better term.

"Just promise me you will consider it, and that we'll discuss it again at a later time."

"No, Alexandros. There is a reason I didn't ask my brothers to finance the deal, and for the same reason, I won't consider this either. I *want* to do this myself, with my own merits and strengths."

"But you have nothing to prove."

"I do." She raised a hand and insisted they finish the discussion. "And I ask that you respect my professional decisions. They are my choices, as respecting them is yours."

Nodding in agreement, Alexandros settled the bill and they began to roam the cobblestone streets where the ancient people once walked. They strolled through the t-shirt shops, dallied by the windows of the traditional jewelry displays, and lingered in the antique stores. Sitting on the steps of a Byzantine church in the area's main square, they shared an ice cream and watched people fill the square. It was a fun afternoon allowing them to explore their pasts and their dreams for the future.

Alexandros pointed to a little gypsy boy dancing with a tambourine in his hands.

"When I was little, I used to tell my father that I wanted to live like the gypsies and play music on the street for a living. I hated wearing shoes, and I thought that would be the way to avoid them."

"I bet that went over well with your father." She laughed at the image of Spiro Strintzaris playing the guitar with the case open at his feet, the way the little boy's father was.

"It only lasted until I was four, then I wanted to be a garbage man and ride on the back of the big trucks." He laughed again, and asked, "What did you want to be when you grew up?"

"I wanted to be a belly dancer. I loved the outfits they wear and the way everything jingles when they move."

"You would be a very enchanting belly dancer, maybe even dangerous. Hey, I could accompany you with my tambourine." He ran his hand down her back and sent shivers up her spine. Bending his head, he placed slightly open lips on the side of her nape in a lingering kiss. "See, you and I can be a very profitable team."

"Well, then puberty hit, and I became aware of my body and physically shy. I focused on my mental attributes and decided I wanted to be a great missionary and save the world. Eventually my nature led me to individual projects of the day that would provide a comfortable living of my choice. By high school, my main requirement was to work in Greece and get paid in dollars." She raised her shoulders in that innately Greek shrug again.

"Smart girl! You can do anything your heart desires, you definitely have the ability." His admiration was obvious as he stood and held a hand out to help her up. "*Pame*, it's almost time to meet with Demosthenis."

Chapter Sixteen

Athena wrapped her arm around Alexandros' back, and his hand gently caressed her bare shoulder as they walked through the gardens. When they approached the cafe, which was their meeting point with her brother, Demo stood and waved at her. He smiled, opening his arms.

She motioned toward him and Alexandros let her go so that she could run into her brother's awaiting embrace. Throwing her arms around his neck, she burrowed into her big brother, and he lifted her in an elaborate bear hug.

"Demo. What a fantastic surprise. I haven't seen you in almost a month. I'm so glad you're here."

"Has it only been a month? It feels more like two years to me. I see a lot of things change in a month." He put her feet back on the ground and kissed her forehead. Then turning, he extended a hand to Alexandros. "Demosthenis Lakis."

Alexandros took the hand, shook it firmly, and in a friendly gesture, covered it with his left hand before speaking. "Alexandros Strintzaris. Very pleased to meet you, Demo."

"What a good coincidence that you should be in Athens today." Demo said, looking from Alexandros to her. "Are you two staying long?"

Demo's eyes focused on Alexandros in a knowing look. Athena could read the mental messages her brother was sending Alexandros.

This is my sister, not a plaything. She is special to me, and you'll do well to honor that.

There was nothing like two macho Greeks meeting for the first time.

"We came in this morning." Alexandros spoke with ease. "We needed to pick up a gift for Heather and take care of some business matters. We thought while we are here, we could not pass up the opportunity for lunch at Thanassi's. The family is expecting us back on the island for dinner late tonight, but I am happy we have the opportunity to get together, if only for this short time."

Alexandros' manner and eyes communicated that he did not intend to *play* with Athena. Demo smiled casually, inviting them to sit as he ordered some frappes from the waiter.

The merger Demo was working on in Zurich had closed early. It'd been a long month, and he'd decided to come ahead of the family to Greece. He explained he wanted some time to refuel before "having Mom parade every potential and suitable Greek wife on Long Island through the house for dinner".

The group laughed and Alexandros added, "Greek mothers, they cannot wait for those grandchildren. Are you the eldest, Demo?"

"Yes, Tony is a year younger, and Athena is our baby." He pinched her with affection. "A big baby now, but still our baby. *Eh, koukla?*"

"How could I ever argue with such a domineering, handsome, and intelligent set of Cretan genes?" Athena rolled her eyes and winked.

"Good, finally someone acknowledges the truth," Demo said, puffing out his chest like a papa penguin and twisting a pretend mustache. "All those tapes I played for her while she was sleeping are finally paying off... *Demo is always right, Demo is fantastic, do as Demo says, Demo is always right, Demo is fantastic* et cetera..."

Holding her abdomen and wiping tears from her eyes, she begged him to stop. Athena took in a breath and let Alexandros in on their private joke. "It was just before second grade when I woke up to such a tape in the middle of night. I laughed so hard I barely made it to the bathroom. He spent an hour repeating the three phrases into a microphone just so I would make his bed for him."

Alexandros raised an amused eyebrow and asked if it had worked.

"Yes, she made my bed everyday for the next four years," Demo said, and laughed.

"That's because you paid me a quarter for each time I did it. Remember?" She rubbed her fingers together for emphasis.

"Do I? You raised it to five dollars a week in fourth grade, and by sixth grade I couldn't afford you anymore." He raised his glass to her.

"Good job, *agape mou*." Alexandros rubbed her shoulder. "I couldn't even get Costa to let me shower in the morning before he did. All I could do was wake up earlier. When it got to be six o'clock, I gave up and took showers at night." The threesome laughed.

"It's only you and Costa?" Demo asked, and Alexandros nodded. "You'll work together now that Costa is back in Greece?" It was more of a statement than a question.

Demo had warned her about Alexandros' professional reputation. He was a smart and effective businessperson. He was feared, but well respected by the international community. When he set his sight on something, he was sure to acquire it. He dotted every 'i' and crossed each 't' without ever resorting to deceitful tactics. Athena knew Demo admired that in a businessperson.

"Yes, I'm looking forward to sharing some of the responsibility. Don't get me wrong, I enjoy what I do, but to have someone I trust implicitly with me is a great advantage."

Demo agreed and told him how he glad he was when Tony had agreed to join him in starting their own international consulting firm.

"It's been only three years, and Lakis Consulting is already a powerhouse in the Greek-American community," Athena added, proud of her brothers. "Simultaneously, they're establishing a very good reputation internationally. Some of the initial investments my brothers made were very fruitful and have increased their net worth into the multi-million dollar category. Joining their energies was very favorable—"

Demo covered her mouth with his palm. "Cut it out. You sound like a walking billboard."

"Well, I look forward to seeing you in the boardroom as well," Alexandros said. Then the conversation left the business world. "Now what about the wedding? You'll be attending, no?"

"I wouldn't miss it. I'll get settled in Crete, and fly out Sunday morning at nine. That gives me enough time to check into a room and come to the church. The wedding is at six if I remember correctly."

"When have you ever been wrong?" Athena wrapped a loving arm through her brother's crooked elbow. "I'll be happy to have more time with you. Can you come earlier?"

"Not really, *koukla*. I have some other things to set up first. I might extend my stay here and work out of Crete this summer. So you'll see me plenty if things work out."

"As for Santorini, there's no need for a hotel. You'll stay with us." Alexandros insisted. "There's plenty of room at *Kalithea*, and it will be a chance for you and I to get better acquainted."

"Done, thank you for the invitation."

They exchanged phone numbers and began to make their way through the gardens.

The sun was low on the horizon and Demo claimed he needed to get to the port—he didn't want traffic to cause him to miss the ferry.

"Do we need anything from the office?" Alexandros asked Athena.

"Just the present and my personal things."

"They're already on the helicopter. It could meet us in Piraeus, that way we could drop Demo at the port since he refuses a ride to Crete with the helicopter."

"Thank you, but that isn't necessary," Demo rejected the suggestion. "I'm meeting Zoe at the garden's entrance. Coincidently, she was heading to Crete for a couple of days and we decided to take the ferry together so we could catch up."

"Zoe? Zoe Marcos?" Athena was surprised. "You two are back together?"

"We never had a falling out. We've known each other since kindergarten. Why don't you like her?"

"Oh please, you two are ridiculous. There is no spark, no fire. You both are guarded and don't want to take a real chance at love. I think you're cowards and don't want to risk being hurt. You've been gravitating towards each other, like people gravitate towards comfort food when they have a hard day. She is not the right woman for you."

"Athena, stop. We're simply taking the boat together, and if you must know, we have separate cabins." Demo gave her a disappointed look. "You are being silly and dramatic. She's a wonderful woman."

"She is wonderful, and I do like her. I've known her all my life and I think of her as a sister. You do too. You're cheating yourself and her by continuing this relationship. You both deserve so much more."

"Since when did my little sister turn into an expert on relationships?" Demo moved closer and gathered her into his arms.

"I promise, I will think about what you said. But only because you are the one who said it. You keep an open mind, and please be polite when you see her. She is really wonderful."

"She is. So is a pair of fuzzy blue slippers."

Demo warned her by raising his eyebrows and giving her a stern look as he spoke. "Don't over do it. I said I would consider what you said. Don't push it any further."

"I'm sorry if I over stepped. I did it because I love you." She snuggled into her brother and kissed him on his tightened jaw. "I just don't want you to eliminate all your other options. I want you to lose your control over a woman who will do the same for you. Just ask yourself if you could live without her. If you can, and we both know you have, she is not the one. If you can lose control over Zoe, then both of you are very lucky people."

Alexandros listened to the siblings intently. He hoped Athena couldn't live without him; he knew he could not live without her.

They spotted Zoe waiting with the car. She did look very beautiful and collected. She walked to Demo and kissed his cheek in greeting. Athena hugged her and introduced her to Alexandros. Zoe seemed very pleasant and sincere in her affections for both siblings. However, he too noticed that there was no flame, no spark between Demo and Zoe. They chatted for a few minutes, asked about the families back in New York, and then bid each other farewell in an amicable fashion.

The Strintzaris building was a short walk away, but instead, Alexandros had a car meet them. He did not tell Athena where they were going, but the car headed in the opposite direction. Alexandros quietly settled her against him and didn't talk.

He was intrigued by the conversation he had been privileged to hear. Her devotion and passion to her brother's happiness had stirred him, and he sat in deep thought, not wanting to disturb her. He would listen when she was ready to talk.

"He really does deserve more you know," she finally said. "I haven't seen Zoe in five years, but I know her very well. She's nice and a good person. We spent a lot of time in each other's homes when we were younger. They were like our extended family."

"Then why don't you want her for your brother? If she is that nice, why is she not good enough for Demo?"

"She would be if he loved her the right way. He loves her the way I do, platonically. As you saw, she's very attractive and I'm sure he has no problem appreciating her body. Who wouldn't like a body like hers?" She looked at him pensively, as if gathering the courage to explain further.

"In college, Zoe was engaged to the love of her life. Patrick was everything to her and he was a great guy. They were together since senior year in high school. Her parents didn't approve of the relationship because he wasn't Greek and he was a catholic. He was one of Demo's friends, so to avoid conflict, Zoe would tell them she was going out with Demo. It wasn't a complete lie, and it worked in high school. In college, they couldn't hide it anymore, and her parents had to accept it.

"Three months before they were to be married, Patrick died in a horrible car accident. We were all devastated. He'd become part of the family. Zoe and Demo took it the hardest. Demo blamed himself for not driving Patrick home after the party, but the truth is that Patrick was not drunk and the accident had nothing to do with his ability to drive himself. Zoe was so depressed she left school and lived in her bedroom for a whole year. She ended up graduating when I was in school, even though she had started with Demo, who was done with school before I was there."

Alexandros listened patiently, rubbing her upper arm gently for support. He knew this was hard for her.

"Patrick's death brought the two of them together, as support for each other. Demo told me that they made an agreement when she graduated. If neither of them were married in ten years, they would marry each other."

"I see." He nodded his head and understood her objection.

"Do you think that is the right reason to get married? Do you think that is enough to base a future on and to build a life without love and passion?" She shook her head side to side answering the questions herself. "Guilt and heartbreak isn't what a marriage needs to survive. Time has passed, and they've both made successes of themselves professionally. If they stop using one another as a shield from the world, they could find the love they deserve."

How did she become so wise? He wanted to tell her it would all work out for her brother. Instead he said, "Demo promised he would think about what you said. And you did give him a lot to think about."

"I know. I hope he isn't angry with me."

"I'm sure he isn't. He can't be angry because you love him and want the best for him. You said what you needed to say, and I'm proud of you for it." He lifted her chin and kissed her. This complex woman stole his heart a piece at a time.

The car made its way up unfamiliar narrow streets for another few minutes. When it halted at what looked like a bus stop, Alexandros opened the door and stepped out.

"Anything else before we head home, *agape mou*?" he asked, offering his hand to help her out.

"The *galaktoboureko*! We nearly forgot."

Alexandros gave the driver instructions to collect the dessert and meet them at the helicopter in forty-five minutes.

She followed him inside what looked like an old bus depot and saw the cable car waiting to carry them up Mount Lycavitos.

"I thought the *teleferique* was not working." She smiled in anticipation.

"It was refurbished and has been operating since last year. Come on. The sun is setting as we speak."

They took the romantic ride to the top and decided to sit on a small bench in the public viewing area to enjoy the view of the city. The sun settled beneath the horizon, and Athens lit up below them. The ancient marble ruins glowed and the city streets shone under twinkling lights.

They abandoned the bench and walked to the other end of the lot to see the rest of the city. He stood behind her and closed his arms beneath her breasts. She leaned her back against his warm chest and sighed with contentment.

"I've always loved spending this time of day here. Today I love it the most because I'm doing it with you." She turned, and for the first time, she kissed him.

The wall between them had fallen and she was comfortable with him. She would not freeze or turn away anymore.

Athena had settled into bed when she heard a soft knock at the door. She heard Alexandros call out and told him to enter. She wasn't expecting him back from dropping off Costa and Heather yet and was unfortunately dressed in a yellow cotton camisole and pink smiley face boxers. Not exactly what she considered sexy lingerie, but she was happy to see him regardless.

"I just wanted to say goodnight properly."

He walked over to the bed and sat on the side. His palm caressed her hair and her heart pounded as he brought his lips to hers. She tasted his minty mouth as he pulled her into his powerful arms. Her breathing grew heavy as she pressed her aching breasts against his hard chest. His hand roamed over her back and down the side of her thigh. Moist warmth spread between her legs, and she held him closer.

"*Kori mou?* Athena?" Anna called from the hallway. "Can I get you anything before I turn in?"

Athena laughed softly as Alexandros slowly pulled away. A sly smile spread across his face and he teased her with his hands. She pushed him, laughing and kicking her legs towards him. He grabbed her right foot and kissed her on the tip of her toes. He pretended to tip his hat, whispered "*kalinihta*", then quietly made his way towards the terrace door.

"No, thank you. *Kalinihta,*" she said, speaking to his mother as she waved her fingers and blew him a silent kiss.

Chapter Seventeen

Athena watched Alexandros help his crew guide the yacht safely out of the harbor as they headed toward the Santorini volcano. After giving final instructions to the captain, he was able to turn all his attention to her.

He came close and pulled her to his side. Her body fit his perfectly.

Pointing out various landmarks, he explained that a local institute was still monitoring the volcano's activity, and that contrary to common belief, there were several volcanoes, not just one.

They spent hours walking the edge of the crater located in the center of the waters surrounding the crescent island. The strong black rock gleamed in the sunlight. It was invigorating to know they had so much power under their feet. Heat rising from the rock seeped into the air, and Athena moved closer to him as they climbed the jutting black peak surrounded by the azure blanket.

Returning to the yacht, they found lunch waiting for them under the canopy. Sitting together on a low couch, they continued talking as they ate. The crew conveniently disappeared, and they relaxed, dreamily discussing the existence of Atlantis below their feet. Natural and right together, it seemed they could just float out there forever.

Suddenly he stopped and turned his body, pulling her against his chest. His arms closed around her.

"I'm very happy to be alone with you."

"I am too," she replied, turning her head to face him.

"I can never forgive Costa for not introducing us earlier," he said, his smile contradicting his severe tone. "You've filled my mind since I met you in Naples, and I've been wanting this moment since then."

"Why didn't you contact me?"

"You avoided me at all costs during the benefit, and I decided to respect your wishes. I didn't want to scare you away." He leaned down and placed a slow line of small kisses behind her ear. He whispered in a husky tone, "Tell me honestly, if I had tried to pursue you, would you have welcomed me?"

"No. I don't think I could have."

"And is that different now?" he asked, hope laced in his dark, velvet voice.

"The thought is much more appealing," she hesitated. "I guess I've gotten to know the person you are, not just the public image."

"My feelings for you haven't changed, they've only grown stronger. I want you more each day."

Alexandros eliminated the small gap between them quickly. Twirling a long finger in a tendril of hair that had escaped her ponytail, his gaze dropped to her mouth.

His lips met hers with the hunger of a man not fed for months, and he wound a possessive arm around her waist as he pulled her onto his lap. He slowly kissed her neck and ran a hand over her heaving breasts. His other hand cupped her buttocks and she rose, arching her body in a natural invitation.

She was letting this go too far, this was not what she'd intended. But she found she no longer cared. She felt right in his arms, she wanted him, and she wanted to be his. For once, she would do want her heart said, not what her rule demanded.

The wind blew an approving caress across them, reminding her that they were exposed to curious eyes on passing boats.

As if he knew her concern, Alexandros stood and carried her across the deck, into the cavernous body of the yacht. She burrowed into him as he took long, swift strides to the end of a corridor, kicking open the door to the master bedroom, then closing it the same way. He carefully arranged her on the bed and then brought his long strong body down on hers.

Her arms reached for his neck, and she tugged him impatiently to her lips. She wrapped her legs around him and felt his excitement when his groin met her thigh.

"Slowly, *yineka mou*. I want to you to feel me on every inch of your skin. I need to savor you," he said, pulling her hair free from the ponytail.

Alexandros ran his hands over her—his *yineka,* his woman. Through her luxurious curls, working his way to her neck. Her charged body filled his fingers as he roamed beneath her shirt and raised it to kiss around her belly button. His hands ascended back toward her neck, lingering over the beautiful full mounds of her breasts. Her breath caught as he exposed the taught, rose peaks and lowered his mouth to one sweet treat, and then the other, simultaneously guiding her shirt over her head.

Running her burning hands over him as she breathed more heat onto his electrified body, Athena entwined her fingers into his hair and asked for his lips against hers. He relished each part of her with tender desire, throwing her into a dizzying tailspin. She raised his shirt, and he fulfilled her need to feel his chest lay across her.

"I will risk my heart," he said. "And I promise to protect yours. I must have you."

She moaned in agreement, and his fingers efficiently unfastened her shorts to allow his hands access. Bracing himself over her, he caressed her gorgeous curves as he lowered the material and pulled it off. He ran his palms along the endless length of her legs, and placed branding kisses on each, marking them as his.

He came back up to the inside of her thighs and his eyes clouded with burning desire. He outlined the white lace panty before slipping his fingers under the soft garment to the curls nestled within. Gently he eased the lace down her legs.

He paused. "Do you know what you do to me?"

Athena pulled his face back to hers and kissed him as her hands moved down to the button of his jeans. Her fingers trembled as she ran her hands inside the back of his jeans pushing them off.

"I hope I do to you what you do to me."

Alexandros ached to immerse himself in her space. He remembered thinking he could put off claiming her as his until the time was right. The time was irrelevant; what was happening here and now was right. Feeling the passion in her touch, hearing it in her voice, and seeing it blaze in her eyes, he knew he was finished waiting. This was it. The moment he'd been waiting for. She was showing him how much she wanted him.

Settling himself between her heavenly thighs, he carefully raised her to him and prepared to join his body and soul with his *yineka*. He enjoyed the taste of her lips in an endless kiss and his eyes held hers, savoring the moment of tenderness preceding their physical union.

She was his, now, today, and tomorrow and *panta*. Forever.

A small, pained moan escaped her mouth as he entered her, and he stilled, terrified he'd hurt her. Searching her face for an indication of her desires, he read her fear, but no hesitation. She was giving herself to him, and he would never let her go. She was his completion.

"Alexandros," she mumbled sensually, pleading with him not to stop.

He carefully adjusted her hips and made slow gentle love to her, devotedly taking her into an abyss she had never known.

Tenderly, he tried to soothe the pain and turn it to ecstasy. He moved just a little closer to the edge of the cliff each time he moved into her core. Determined to make her first time blissful, he slowly encouraged her body's surrender to the intense pleasure. When he felt her wrap still tighter around him, her body calling out to his, he joined her, releasing himself deep within her.

He dropped his face into her hair and covered her body with the protection he had promised. She was the missing piece of the puzzle from his life, and now that he'd found her, he wasn't going to let her go. He would make her happy. He'd earn her love—regardless of how much more patience he'd need.

She tried to talk, but he silenced her lips with his. One way or another, he'd show her she was his. To have. To protect. To love.

It was his last thought before the movement of the sea lulled them both to sleep, still entangled in their passionate embrace.

Athena awoke to the soft touch of his lips on her eyelids. *"Agape mou*, we're back in port and we have two hours before the party." He bent, kissing her sleepy lips. They'd missed the scuba diving.

"I...I slept." She hesitated opening her eyes.

"You needed it," he insisted. "The fresh air and water are very tiring, and you're still recovering from yesterday in Athens. We've had a pretty active day."

Raising teasing eyes, he kissed her open palm, and intensely met her gaze. She recalled the afternoon she had just shared with him and her cheeks burned, while she drew an image of herself with cheeks of red peppers in her mind.

He continued, "You're more of a hooligan than you appear to be."

She raised a brow in question.

"You broke your rule, and now you are romantically involved with a Greek, a very fortunate one, dare I point out, on your summer vacation."

She froze, felt the blood drain from her face. What had she done? How had she let this happen? She was supposed to be in control. She cursed softly under her breath.

He was still talking, "and as I warned you yesterday, I'm very difficult to shake off." He kissed her trembling mouth and pulled her into him.

You will not be when you find out this is the extent of my sexual experience. Then you will forget my name.

Her body fought her mind, but her mind prevailed. She jumped out of bed, and began to search for her clothes.

"Let's get back to your family before they start having inappropriate thoughts."

"I think they are very appropriate. You cannot hide something like this from people who love you." Coming to stand beside her, he took her shoulders, and said, "Remember, I want you proud to be with me."

Tears welled behind her eyes and she lowered them. "I don't think this was a good idea, Alexandros."

He looked as if she had just slapped him.

"I mean, I'm not very good at this, and I don't know what to do or how to act."

"You're doing just fine. What do you mean how to act?" He wasn't letting her sulk into her own thoughts.

"Alexandros, you're the first man I've ever been wi—"

He silenced her, placing a strong finger on her swollen lips. "Yes, I know, and I cherish the gift you have bestowed on me with all my heart. No one can predict what tomorrow brings, but as for today, you are here, with me, right now." A territorial light burned in his eyes.

She looked away. One could not predict tomorrow, but one could prepare for the worst-case scenario.

"Don't ask me to leave, and do not worry about inexperience. *Agape mou*, I swear, what we share is not common. Our passion and chemistry is not something learned from experience. We either have it, or we do not. We do, and we will learn the rest together."

She stared at him and wondered what he had to *learn*.

He laughed. "I won't pretend to be innocent, but we will discover together what we want from each other. I think we are doing very well for beginners."

"I don't want any misunderstandings. I can't ruin my relationship with the family." A tear slipped down her cheek.

"Thee mou!" He looked angry. "Why can't you just trust what we have? What do you think I will do?" His gaze narrowed. "Do you think I'm a callous monster? That I do not have a heart?"

Athena turned her back to him and attempted to dress. She didn't know how to respond.

"Don't pull away from me, *agape mou*. I'm not going to lose you, not now. I know you feel the same way I do. You felt it the very first time we met, just as I did. I'll fight for you."

He turned her to look straight into her eyes and adjusted his tone. "I don't want to hurt or shame you, but do not dare ask me to act as if this never happened. We have no one but ourselves to answer to on this matter."

She kept watching his lips move. Tearing apart inside, she ached for him to hold her together. He did.

"Knowing that no other man has been where I have makes me treasure what we have more. I want to keep you closer to me. I want you so much. I cannot walk away. No sane man could leave you after making love the way we did. The way we do."

He guided her back onto the bed and sealed her mouth with his. She did not resist him. She could not. She arched her body to accept him and he entered where no other man had been. He possessed her body and heart, sending her quickly spiraling.

He was not gentle, nor was he was slow. He took her with raw, vulnerable passion, challenging her to send him away.

Just before they both climaxed, he asked, "Why would you deny us?"

She cried out as waves of pleasure washed over her trembling form.

When the waves subsided, she looked into his eyes, and saw her soul. She decided to put her fears aside. "I will risk my heart too."

He didn't respond. But before returning to the house, they made love again, this time, soft and tender.

They arrived at *Kalithea* with little time to spare before the party. They discreetly rushed up the stairs and into their respective rooms through the veranda doors. Athena bathed, did her hair, and was stepping into a strapless blue dress when he entered her room.

"Just in time to help," she said, offering her back to be zippered. Her inhibitions had faded. She'd made the decision to trust, and now she allowed herself the comfortable intimacy between them. She gave herself to the feelings that swelled in her chest. Her heart beat a little faster as she anticipated his touch.

His fresh masculine scent surrounded her as he approached and fitted his hips against her buttocks, and then dropped his shoulders so that his arms could encircle her middle. She loved the feel of his body on hers.

"Maybe we should skip the party," he said, snuggling into the crook of her neck "We can make our own here." Alexandros brushed his lips over her bare shoulders. "They won't miss us. It's just a big family barbecue," he rationalized.

She was in the arms of the most entrancing man she had ever met. His breath caused the hair on the back of her neck to stand and heat to spread into her abdomen, igniting something new. Desire, hunger, fear… love?

Realizing she was his, that she had given herself completely to him, she felt vulnerable, exposed, and truly ecstatic to be his. Pulling away, she laughed and reached for her stiletto sandals.

"A bit of lipstick and I'll be ready," she called heading for the bathroom.

When she returned, she saw his eyes full of adoration.

"It takes most women hours to look half as beautiful as you do in only a few minutes," he complimented.

Alexandros tenderly kissed her bronzed cheek, interlaced her arm through his, and led her to the waiting car. They drove to the Strintzaris inland estate.

Chapter Eighteen

Athena walked through the domed entrance into the traditionally decorated living room, observing the crowd that buzzed throughout the illuminated villa. The mass of people gradually moved towards the terrace, kissing everyone in greeting on the way.

Lanterns twinkled atop white tablecloths, welcoming young and old to feast on the spread of *mezedes* that adorned the tables. The guests talked loudly, laughter filling the night air. They clinked glasses of *nikteri*, white wine from grapes picked before dawn, and red *vissanto*. The dance floor was already starting to fill with the enthusiastic family members.

This was not a backyard barbecue. It was a *panygiri*, a festival and a rite of celebration. She stared at the magnificence of the family's interactions and was not able to speak.

Alexandros moved his hand to her hip. "Did I tell you how gorgeous you are?"

"You have a large, loud family," Athena said, admiring the two hundred people below her.

"My father is one of five children, my mother one of eight. All my aunts and uncles are married with children of their own, many of them with children as well. I guess you could say we're a large family. As for the loud part, all I can say is we're Greeks."

A little mass of flowery curls bound out at them, entwining her hands jubilantly around his thigh. She spoke in bumbling Greek. "*Theo*, what took you so long? I've been waiting to show you my *kalamatiano*."

Alexandros pulled his tiny niece into his big arms, lavishing her face with kisses. He did it with such natural ease, once again surprising Athena with the warmth and love he gave to the people in his life.

"Mommy taught me the steps for the wedding dance." She placed a loud, smacking kiss on his mouth and hugged her uncle very tight. The little girls fingers wound into his hair as she looked sweetly into his face. "Is this pretty lady your bride, *Theo?*"

Athena knew she'd blushed to the roots of her hair. Feeling her face ablaze, she blinked and tried to deflect the question. "The bride is Heather. Your *Theo Costa* is dancing with her. See?" She pointed to the dance floor.

The little bundle of dark curls opened her twinkling eyes wide, and then scrunched her nose at her uncle in question.

"This is *my* Athena," he said, nudging his nose into the little girl's neck. "Do you like her?"

"Will you dance *kalamatiano* with me?" the little girl asked Athena. When Athena smiled and nodded in agreement, the girl gave a decisive nod of her own. "Yes, I like her."

Alexandros laughed loud and winked to Athena. "You've probably guessed Lexi is the shy, quiet girl of the family." He placed the little girl on the floor, playfully swatting her behind. "Go practice, *koukla,* I can't wait to see such a pretty girl dance."

He returned to Athena and gave her a quick, yet sensuous, kiss. His eyes began to undress her, and he ran his open palm wantonly over her back. She put her hands against his chest and pushed him a few inches away warning.

"*Semna....semna*, Alexandros."

"Okay, I'll be a little more discreet," he said. His lips brushed hers again and his gaze locked on hers. "Only if, you agree to go home with me tonight."

"Like I have a choice. That's where I'm staying."

"Yes, that is where you are staying, in my room, in my bed, in my arms," he said, fueling the flame inside her before softly adding, "*panta.*"

"Athena this is *Thea* Marianna, *Thea* Marianna, Athena." Warm embraces and a duet of kisses followed each introduction.

"*Theo* Manoli, cousin Costa, *Thea* Georgia, Maria, Anna, Gianni…"

The faces and names ran together. They were so many and she was only one. The one on Alexandros' arm who inspired the young girls to giggle, the women to smile, and the mature men to nod in approval.

Exhausted from the past hour, Athena walked to the balustrade of the large terrace. She ran her fingers over the thick white plaster and thought to herself how funny life was. Yesterday, she was determined to be a little more than friends with Alexandros. Today, she was immersed in his family, proud to be the woman on his arm.

He was everything she'd ever wanted in a man. He was strong, powerful, tender and funny. He was loyal and in turn, commanded loyalty from others. He loved the people around him, protected the people he loved. Oh, what she would not give to be one of those people?

She'd been wrong. She had to give this a chance. He could be her future. She wanted him to be her future.

"Would you like a drink?" Alexandros placed a champagne flute in her hand. He stood behind her, wrapping her in his arms, and looking out over the vineyard. "What are you thinking, *agape mou*?"

She laid her head back on his shoulder, marveling how well her body fit his. She had been so wrong about him, and she was so happy to have discovered her mistake. Exhaling deep, she closed her eyes, hoping this moment would go on forever.

"*Agape mou*?" he repeated.

"I was just thinking," she said, turning to look up at his handsome face.

His eyes sparked with desire. He brought his head down and parted her lips, gently trailing his tongue across her teeth. Spreading his fingers as if to feel as much of her as he possibly could, he pulled her tight against him, and crushed her breasts to his chest.

"*Semna*," she warned. Still conscious of the family surrounding them, her good sense had not abandoned her and cautioned against such sensuous exhibitions of their feelings.

He grinned and licked his lips. "Are you having a good time?"

"A very good time. Your family is amazing. They are such warm, passionate, and loving people." She added silently, *they are people I would gladly welcome into my life.*

An attractive young man approached holding out his hand. "Athena, would you like to dance?"

"I would be honored." She smiled at Alexandros and took the other man's hand as he led her to the dance floor.

Alexandros joined the big circle two songs later. With hands linked to shoulders, they let the music guide them in the whirlwind of moving people.

The band picked up the tempo, persuading the participants to kick fiercely as the ritual progressed. One by one, dancers conceded to the fast pace, leaving Alexandros, Costa, cousin Gianni, and cousin Spiro to prove they could outlast the musicians.

It was exhilarating to watch the men move in perfect synchrony. Swift, sure feet pounding, arms locked in wartime severity, and bodies bending at the waist to claim the dance floor as theirs.

The band challenged the dancers by quickening the beat, the dancers responded by moving faster, adding more intricate steps. The spectators held their breaths, clapping in unison, faster, stronger, quicker, louder… it kept building to the climactic end when the four men jumped through the air, landing on their knees at the edge of the dance floor.

Heather ran into Costa's arms giving him an exaggerated squeal. "Now that is what I call macho!" The group burst into laughter, and raising their glasses, toasted to the night.

Lexi bounced over to Athena exclaiming, "The *kalamatiano* is now, are you coming?" Athena took the little girl's hand and joined the group of new dancers.

Alexandros was watching Athena and Lexi weave through the erected wooden floor when his cellular rang. She caught his gaze, he winked, stood, and on the next turn was gone.

She continued to dance until it was time for Lexi to go home. "You're a great dancer, *koukla*," she said, giving Lexi a goodnight kiss.

"You too," said the little girl kissing Athena twice. "One for you, and one for *Theo*." Waiving goodbye, she followed her parents up the stairs.

Athena imagined Alexandros' little girl would look just like Lexi. Loose dark curls, full little pink lips against a smooth olive complexion, and big chocolate almond eyes that would melt her Daddy's heart as her little hands encircled his neck for more kisses.

She took a deep breath, filling her lungs with the cool island air. Athena saw Yiayia Maria motioning her to come and sit beside her. She walked over to the older woman and sat.

"Are you having a good time, *kori mou*?"

"Wonderful."

"You've enticed our family. They think you're wonderful."

"Thank you. The feeling is mutual."

The grandmother smiled and took Athena's hand between her own. "I believe the feeling is mutual for my Alexandros too?"

Athena was speechless.

"Don't be surprised. I'm old, not blind. I see the love his eyes hold when he looks at you. I also see your eyes when you look at him. I like what I see."

"But Yiayia, we've just met. We should not put the carriage ahead of the horse." Athena suddenly felt exposed.

"*Kori mou*, you're in Santorini. We have donkeys, not horses. Stubborn, hard headed donkeys!" Athena laughed and Yiayia smiled. "You don't have to say anything, just listen."

Yiayia's fingers lovingly caressed Athena's hands as she spoke. "The Strintzaris men have never kept to any conventional time table. They decide when and how; we have just been blessed to agree with them. Alexandros is a good man. Everything he does, he does with zeal. You may not realize it yet, but in these hands, you hold Alexandros' heart. Cherish it, love it and he will be good to you, loving you forever."

"Yiayia, I know he is a good man. He's strong, loyal, and tender with his family. It shows how much he loves you all. As for us, we… we are getting to know each other." Athena struggled to get the last words out.

"No. Alexandros has no traditional timetable. He wants to make you his. Personally, I'm very happy. Look in your heart, child. You are not a girl that easily decides to simply 'get to know' a man, throw caution to the wind, and trust him for only now. But that is good, very good. You and Alexandros will complete each other."

She continued to hold Athena's hands. "Humor an old lady. Please remember that no matter how strong a man is, he gets that strength from a woman's love and support."

Deep in silent thought, they watched the lantern on the table flicker.

"*Kori mou*, you will see what is right in front of us." Yiayia exhaled loudly.

This wise woman was correct and it scared Athena.

She loved him.

She wanted to be his, and she wanted him to be hers. Hers to love and to cherish. She craved his touch, his arms around her to assure her. Searching the crowd, she asked, "Yiayia, do you see him?"

The older woman waggled her eyebrows and chuckled. "Go to him, *kori mou*. He is inside the house."

Athena stood and gratefully squeezed Yiayia's hand, before ascending the stairs to the main floor. She stepped into a room with a mirror to adjust her dress and check her hair. Her reflection verified what she was feeling. The flame inside her burned hot. Color filled her face and her eyes twinkled. She was in love. Elated by the truth, she was not going to deny it.

Her heart raced when she glimpsed Alexandros at the end of the hall. Then she heard him speak to someone and stopped short, holding her breath.

"I'm so glad you made it," he said. "It's been so hard waiting all night for the ring of the phone."

"Alexandros, don't you know, I would do anything for you?" A sultry female voice stung Athena's ears.

"You're truly one of a kind." He passed in front of the door, and Athena saw the green skirt sway beside him. "Come, privacy is assured in here."

Athena looked into the hallway; saw his hand in the small of the other woman's back guiding her into a bedroom. The door closed and locked behind them.

Her heart shattered, splintered into jagged little pieces cutting her apart. She was bleeding profusely and could not breathe. She ran out the room, out the main entrance, away from him.

Chapter Nineteen

Athena's feet skimmed over the stone steps as she ran away from the house and into the garden. She wanted to go anywhere, anyplace far away from Alexandros, but she had no place to go. She felt trapped, with no car, no taxi, not even a donkey. She was in the middle of a rock and had no place to hide.

Her stomach curdled and emptied its contents, the taste of hell filling her mouth.

"I hate you, Alexandros Strintzaris," she cried. "I hate you for making me believe you were more than the others."

Liar! He was worse than the others! At least they did not pretend. Women came seeking a summer fling, a sexual encounter on a majestic island, and the Greek men obliged. She had seen it many times. Once the interlude was over, they parted contently, beginning the next dance with another partner.

Alexandros Strintzaris had misled her. He had used her. He could have had any other willing woman on the island. Why had he insisted on humiliating her?

She'd told him she was not looking for a week's sensual release. Now it would cost her dearly. How could she ever sit with her friends knowing what he could say?

Clamping her hands on the sides of her whirling head, she screamed into the empty garden.

Why should she hide? He was the one who had hurt her. He had not even waited twenty-four hours to make love to another woman. They had been together less than five hours ago. She had not left the island yet. He was supposed to wait until she left the island to replace her.

Athena's chin trembled as she struggled to contain her tears. She could play the game as well as anyone. Heather's dream wedding would not be ruined. They'd never know how she felt. She'd turn the tables on him and show him that she did not care. He too could be replaced.

"Get control of yourself. You knew this was going to happen. You let it happen because you broke your rule."

The words shattered the night, stark and raw with her pain. Only she did not want to believe them. She'd trusted him. She loved him.

Her legs could not carry her any further, and they dropped her in the garden. Tears stung her eyes as she brought her knees to her chest and began to cry.

Within moments, Spiro Strintzaris yelled to her, "*Kori mou*, what is wrong? Are you hurt?"

Freezing like a deer in headlights, Athena could barely see through her tears. She could not speak.

"Athena!" He grabbed her shoulders and shook her. "*Kori mou,* speak to me." The alarm in his voice dimmed those headlights.

"I'm okay." She looked into his eyes, the eyes he had given Alexandros, and started to cry. "Please, I need to be alone," her voice faded into the tears.

The big man sat on the ground beside her and opened his arms. "Come here. Let me help you, please."

She let his arms close around her shoulders as she lowered her head into his chest and wept. He stroked her hair, kissed the top of her head, and spoke to her in a calming voice. "*Kori mou,* how can I take away your hurt? Tell me why you're upset. What can I do to make it better?"

Athena just stared. She couldn't tell him.

"*Paidi mou,* did someone bother you?" Spiro's voice was strained. "Please talk to me. I want to help, and you're tying my hands. Did anyone touch you?"

She had to tell him. This poor man thought someone had physically abused her. "No, nothing like that. I made a bad decision and abandoned my beliefs. It'll cost me dearly now."

"*Kori mou,* don't let a bad decision upset you so. We can fix it if you tell me what went wrong."

"I don't know how it could be fixed." She was controlling her sobs. "I have to leave. I want to be alone to think."

"Okay, *paidi mou.* Do not cry. We can easily arrange for you to leave the party. I will call Alexandros to take you home if you wish."

"No!" The harshness in her voice shocked even her.

He held her at arm's length and studied her away face with the patience of a father soothing his young child.

She regained control and pleaded, "Not Alexandros. I do not want to go with him. I don't want to go to Villa *Kalithea.*"

"*Kori mou*, please tell me what has happened." Spiro's eyebrows drew together and formed an angle over his nose. He took a long time to speak again. "I cannot understand this. You were so happy a few minutes ago."

She sat silently, but refused to talk. She let him place his arms around her trembling shoulders again, her body shaking with sobs she was burying in his chest.

"Please, *kori mou*," he urged for her to look at him. Locking his palms around her face, he wiped her tears, his sincerity touching her soul. "You have my word, I will stand by you, and I will not betray your confidence. I just want to help. You must let me help."

"He is inside making love to a woman…the green gown," she began shaking all over again.

"Who? I don't understand."

"Alexandros" she cried. "He is with this woman in the bedroom—he—he said he was so happy to see her."

"*Paidi mou*, are you sure? Maybe you misheard. Perhaps you are mistaken."

She shook her head.

"I know my son, as I know my own hand, he loves you. He has never shown any affection, no matter big or small, for any other woman but you in front of the family. He doesn't hide his feelings for you. He wears them proudly on his sleeve."

"No, Mr. Strintzaris, I'm not mistaken. I saw him. Heard him. He told her they would have privacy in the room, and then he locked the door."

"*Dropi!*" Spiro replied, his voice a mixture of shame and anger. "How could my son do this to you? And here in my home! I will find out the truth. There must be an explanation."

His words made her sob more. Now his father was angry.

"Athena, do you want to stay here tonight?"

"No, I want to be alone. I need to get my things from *Kalithea*, and I will leave. I really want to go away."

"You cannot do that, *kori mou*. You are in my care until the day of the wedding. You cannot leave until you go to Crete for work. We have some rental property on the eastern part of the island. I will arrange for you to stay in the holiday cabanas until I find what has happened."

He kissed her forehead and helped her to her feet. Walking toward the house, he told her the driver would drop her off tonight, she would find the necessities in the bungalow and he would take care of this. He stopped in front of the entrance and asked her to wait for him to return.

Athena paced the drive. Her shoulders drawn against her torso to shield the pain. The sound of Alexandros' voice froze the blood in her veins.

"I've been looking everywhere for you. What is wrong, *agape mou*?"

Agape mou! He had no right. She turned to stare up into Alexandros' face.

"Do not dare *agape mou* me!" The venom in her eyes stung. "It was fun, now leave me alone."

She turned to hide her tears, feeling him come up behind her and grasp her shoulders. She jerked at his touch. "You know my rule. Now leave me alone!" she shouted. "Just go back to what you were doing."

Alexandros dropped his hands and balled his fists at his side. He was not sure he could control himself. He would never hit a woman, but he wanted to shake her until she took back those despicable words.

Clenching his teeth, he grabbed a hold of her arm and swung her around.

"Your rule. Eh? The rule that a Greek is not good enough for you! Is it regrets that plague you? Well look in the mirror and see what you are!"

"I know what I am. A fool." She twisted out of his hold and walked away from him. "Look, it's nothing personal, we had fun, but now I have things to do. I must go. Please go back the party."

"I don't care about the party! What is wrong with you?" Alexandros couldn't believe what he heard spill from her lips. It was illogical.

He approached her again. She jumped. He stopped. Frightening her was not his intention. But he couldn't keep the anger from building as his eyes burned, and he tried to recognize the woman standing in front of him. "We need to talk."

"Alexandros." She spoke his name as if it hurt her.

"What is wrong with you? What's happened?" Running his hand over his face, he stalked toward her and began to raise his voice. Looking into her eyes, he could see her mind devising a plan. "And don't lie to me. I want the truth."

"The truth? You want the truth?" She raised her chin and spoke directly to his face.

She was distraught and he wanted to take her pain away, to make it better.

"Athena, I don't know what's happened, but please let me take you home and we'll–" A cold chill traveled down his spine as a horrific thought occurred to him. Immediately, against her will, he took her into his arms and held her against his chest.

"Is Giorgios here?"

"No. What gave you that idea?"

"Then, what is wrong? You look as if you've lost a loved one, or you've been horribly hurt. And you are angry with me for no reason. What am I supposed to think?"

"No, no. It's nothing like that." She softened her voice and skimmed her fingers over his solid forearm. "Please don't ruin the party for Costa and Heather. We'll talk later."

"Okay, let's go home. We'll talk there, now." He took hold of her arm.

"Please say goodnight first. Please, for me."

He could not believe her. Say goodnight? His priority was with her, but he did not want to fight any more.

"Wait here, I will be right back."

She sighed as he strode into the house, glancing over his shoulder to check on her.

"Goodbye Alexandros," she whispered, a tear escaping her eye.

Spiro came down the stairs as the car pulled up. Handing her an overnight bag, he said, "Eleni keeps some clothes here, they should fit. I have put my cell phone and some money in the bag. Call me if you need me before I call you tomorrow. I promise to get to the bottom of this, fix it and to let you know."

"There is nothing for you to let me know. However, I am grateful to you. Goodnight," she said in a shaky voice.

"*Kalinihta, kori mou.*" He brushed his lips across her temple and helped her into the car.

Athena could see the cabana on the black sandy beach. Someone had preceded them and turned on the lights. It was a little glow in the vast darkness. The driver insisted on walking her to the door, placing the overnight bag in the small bedroom, and adjusting the climate control unit before leaving.

"Miss Athena, please use the climate control at night. We have never had any problems, however it is very dark on the beach for a woman alone."

"Thank you, I'll be fine."

"There's a basket with bread on the counter, and a few things in the refrigerator for the morning. Fifty yards up the road is a small store for anything else you may need. Makis runs the *taverna* next to them and has the best calamari on the island. Mr. Spiro has alerted them of your arrival. They are expecting you tomorrow."

"Thank you." She just wanted him to leave. She didn't care about any of this. All she wanted was to get into to bed, close her eyes, and make it all go away.

The driver studied the expression on her face and hesitated. Could he tell something was tearing at her? That she was not here for a pleasant beach holiday, and she was running from something or someone?

"Miss Athena, the cabana has no phone. Please hold mine."

She assured him she had a phone and she felt very comfortable alone on the beach. Besides, the other bungalows appeared occupied. She would be fine.

He walked to the kitchen counter, telling her his name was Demosthenis. He wrote his number on a pad, and asked her to call him if she should have the need.

"Thank you, Demosthenis. Goodnight." She closed the door behind him, placed her back against it, and slowly sank to the floor.

His name was Demosthenis. Just like her brother's. What would she do when her Demo arrived? How could she have been such an idiot?

The tears lost no time returning, burning her cheeks as they rolled. She had lost control, was spent and slept where she had landed.

Chapter Twenty

Alexandros was baffled. Where was Athena?

His fingers strained the steering wheel as he turned the car into *Kalithea's* drive. He made it up the stairs in four swift strides only to find her room empty for the second time tonight.

She was still on the island. She had not left from any of the three airports and could not tonight. There were no more outbound flights. The last ferry had sailed at midnight, and the next would not depart until tomorrow afternoon.

No one was at *Cardia Mou*, and he was alone. Perhaps he had not seen her when he searched for her at the party. Maybe she had decided to stay there with Costa and Heather. He picked up the phone and dialed.

"*Ne?*" His father's sleepy voice answered.

"Baba, sorry to wake you."

"Is everything all right?" Spiro asked, sounding alarmed, no doubt because of the time.

"Baba, is Athena with you?"

"No." Spiro hesitated as if contemplating his answer. "She is safe though."

"Where is she?"

No answer. Silence filled the line.

"Baba, the last time I saw her she was not okay. She was upset and made no sense."

"Can you honestly blame her?"

What was his father alluding to? What had he missed that had upset everyone? Alexandros' body tightened with each thought, feeling as if his shoulder would separate from his neck at any moment.

"Listen, *paidi mou*, you need to let her rest. She cannot bear anymore pain tonight."

Pain! A piercing fear rammed his mind.

"What is wrong?" Alexandros demanded, struggling to get the words out.

"I'm your father, no matter what you do I will always love you, but I do not condone what you did." Spiro spoke with the controlled voice he'd used when he'd lectured him as a boy.

There was no mistaking how his father felt. He held Alexandros responsible for Athena's condition. The younger Strintzaris remained quiet and waited for his father to complete his thought.

"I cannot understand why. No, I loathe what you did. I thought I raised you better than that, Alexandros."

Had the whole world gone mad?

"Baba. I don't understand."

"Athena saw you. She saw you go into the bedroom and lock the door. It was not right, *paidi mou*."

"Why was it not right? I'm a man who knows what he wants, and I intend to get it! What is wrong with that? You, of all people, should understand that."

"*Dropi!*" The older man said. "I will not continue this conversation with you. You are wrong. Do not call back till you realize that!"

The phone slammed, killing the connection.

Alexandros stared at the receiver in disbelief.

Well, at least she was safe. He trusted his father would not leave her alone. She needed to rest he said, no more pain tonight…

His tight chest heaved as he tried to understand why they would be so upset.

I want to make Athena mine forever. Everything else is irrelevant, petty and ridiculous.

He walked into her room, stripped off his clothes, and went to shower. A quick, cold shower only stressed his body more. Finished, he stretched out on the bed he had held her in, the bed where he had learned that he could not put off making her his for a minute longer. With his hands crossed under his head, he stared at the ceiling until sunrise.

Pulling back the sheet with her sweet scent embedded in it, he tried to roll the tension out of his neck. She should be there with him. How could she be blind to his need for her, her need for him? His mind was not clear. He needed to think.

He made a coffee, and took it to the little blue table. Mindlessly swirling the coffee, he gazed out over the caldera.

Her eyes speak her love, her body heats at my touch, yet she runs from me. It doesn't make sense. Athena knows the real me. I didn't hide anything from her. I'm no longer someone she just met at the ball and rightfully should not trust.

Recalling their conversation, his brain clicked. His gut tightened, and he mentally chastised himself for not realizing his mistake. His father was right. He had made a mistake. His actions had been rash and didn't consider her reactions. Now, she was not with him.

Days ago, she had told him she did not wish to be involved with a Greek. He'd insisted, as was only natural, and when she had acknowledged what they had between them, he had assumed it would not matter that he was a Greek. He didn't care where she was from, what passport she carried, as long as she was his.

Did he expect her to change her whole life to accommodate him on such short notice? This was too much to ask of her. He'd assumed she would move to Greece, leave her job, and be the center of the universe, as he knew it.

That had to be what had hurt her, the inconsiderate assumptions. He knew what to do. He would fix it.

With great optimism, he dressed and ran down the stairs. The car was speeding to his parents' house in minutes. He would make her see, she would agree, and he would have her forever.

Invigorated, he pressed down on the gas pedal, allowing the cool morning to fill his lungs with renewed confidence as he traveled to his destination. Thinking of her understanding his impatience and walking beside him at the wedding tomorrow, he smiled to himself.

Alexandros strolled through the door calling out a greeting.

"*Kalimera*. Where are you?"

"On the back patio, *paidi mou*," Anna replied.

He walked to the patio with a light step in his heart. He was going to fix this now, and put an end to the pain. It was done. Seeing his parents eating breakfast, he bent to kiss his mother's cheek, and sat beside them.

"Would you like some coffee?"

"No, but I'd like a word with Baba."

Anna glimpsed Spiro's grim gaze and left the two men alone. His father refused to speak.

"Baba, where is she? I need to see her."

"No, *paidi mou*. I gave her my word she would be left alone." Spiro rubbed his forehead and shook his head. He looked tired, as if he hadn't slept well.

"I need to talk with her. I know what to do to make everything right."

"You were wrong." The older man turned hopeful eyes to his son, scrutinizing him.

"Yes, and I regret putting her through any turmoil. It hurts me so much to know that I caused her pain. I was being very selfish by putting my needs before hers, and I regret it. I can't stand to lose her. No matter what it takes to make it right, I'll do it."

"Alexandros, I believe you're sincere and your heart is hurting, but I cannot understand why you acted as you did. Until you just admitted it, I thought, I hoped, there'd been some mistake. Now my hand is forced. I must keep my word and honor the girl's wish of privacy."

Dumbfounded, Alexandros sat in silence. What had come over his father? "What's the big deal? My actions are insignificant in the larger scheme of things?"

"Insignificant? No, Alexandros. Have I ever given you the impression that women are to be anything other than cherished and respected?"

"No. You haven't. But Father, I do respect her, and I intend to cherish her with every breath I have. I love her. I want to make her my wife. I never meant to hurt her or disrespect her wishes. Now, I understand that I was wrong to assume that I could do what pleases me without considering her reaction. It'll never be an issue again."

Spiro nodded his head and sighed. He took his son's hand and looked directly into his eyes. "I believe you. But you must give her time and prove your sincerity. She may not be able to forgive you. You acted recklessly, and I never thought of you as a tactless man. I question your readiness to commit to Athena."

This was outrageous. He needed to find her. "Please Baba, tell me where she is."

"No, she needs time to heal. I gave her my word."

"This is ridiculous!" Alexandros was out of patience. He stood up and slammed his hand on the table. "I cannot understand you, but I will not sit here and argue with you anymore. Tell her I am looking for her." He began heading for the car. "You know I will find her."

The tires spun as Alexandros pulled the car onto the main road.

His father knew where she was, he was being unreasonable, and it did not make any sense. He had acknowledged his mistake, admitted he had been selfish. Why was his father acting as if he had committed a carnal sin?

The bright light woke Athena. She rubbed her thighs and stretched her stiff neck. Her whole body was sore, her head pounded, and her heart ached. She slowly rose to her feet, took in a deep breath, and swallowed the rancid taste lingering in her mouth.

Walking into the bedroom, she longed to forget last night. She unzipped her dress, letting it drop to the floor before she climbed into the bed. Breathing hurt, her chest constricted, and her eyes burned from the tears.

You put yourself in this predicament! You allowed him to enter her heart, and you didn't play by the rule.

She should've avoided him, and seen him for the egotistical playboy she knew he was.

Athena thought of the past few days. She'd let her guard down, and had easily fallen for the smooth charisma Alexandros possessed. Smart, he had not used his usual playboy skills on her knowing they would not have worked. Rather he amused himself and passed his time portraying a sincere and genuine man who was so addicting to be with.

He'd promised to protect her heart.

Instead, he'd shattered it.

Just as it had been shattered so many years ago. She had been barely fourteen on a beach in Crete when she had overheard her sixteen-year old crush, Nikos, laying bets on how fast he would get the *Americanaki* to bed. He had made crude remarks about her tempting little body and the sexual experience of girls like her. "Girls like her are easy. She'll do everything."

She had been devastated.

She had gone home and straight to bed, supposedly for an afternoon nap. Her brother, Demo, had found her crying when he had returned from the beach. He had patiently tried to console her for over hour, finally he was able to get her to tell him the reason for her tears. He'd held and rocked his sister until she had fallen into a peaceful sleep.

When Athena had awakened, she had felt better from the soothing words her brother had whispered to her. She'd gone to sit with her family on the balcony, and saw Demo with an ice pack on his swollen eye.

"Demo, what happened?" she'd gasped in horror.

"Not too much." He'd raised his shoulders just a bit. "I met up with Nikos at the café and…You can see the rest."

"I'm so sorry. This is all my fault," she'd cried.

"*Stamata!* Stop right now. It's not your fault. Anyway, even Nikos knows he was wrong to speak those disgusting things about you. Now go get ready, we're going to the *taverna* to meet up with everyone."

"I can't. Demo, I cannot face any of them. They heard what he said, and I'm so embarrassed. I can't believe I thought he was a nice guy. I feel ashamed that I even had a crush on him."

"Athena, please go get ready. Come to the *taverna* with me. After all, I'm the one with the humongous eye, not you, *koukla mou.*"

Demo had played his trump card: he'd called her his doll, as he had since they were toddlers. He'd then pointed out his eye had taken a beating, not hers. She felt obligated into accompanying her brother anywhere he wanted to go.

They had arrived at the *taverna* and sat at the table with friends from the beach. Nikos had come in looking much worse off than her brother. He'd stood before her and had apologized publicly for the things he'd said. Admitting he had not meant to hurt her, but had been trying to showoff to his friends, all of which were privileged to his apology. Nikos cried in front of her. He had not left until Demo told him to go, and then he had done so with his tail tucked between his legs.

It may have been childish, but the whole experience had soured Athena on any romantic ideas with Greeks. She associated every Greek man with her teenage crush. She had lost her trust in them. That, and her observance of the summer romances that blossomed and wilted around her each year, had extinguished all romantic flames for her.

Tomorrow Demo would come to Santorini, and what would she tell him? He had seen her together with Alexandros in Athens. Her brother was not dumb, and he knew how she felt about Alexandros. Even worse, if she told him what had happened, it would ruin her best friend's wedding for sure. She had to think of what to do, perhaps keep him from coming to the island.

What she found the most peculiar was that Demo had not seen through Alexandros. He was usually a good judge of character, and he seemed to have approved of the relationship. Well obviously, Alexandros was an excellent actor, or simply had his morals all twisted and hidden. She'd been fooled.

She'd thought Alexandros was different. She'd believed the press had used him to sell papers, when in reality he had used her to fill his time.

He'd made a strong and compelling game of pursuing her, and she had been inept enough to believe him. Imagining he cared about her, not just her body, not just for the week, she'd opened her heart to him. She'd allowed herself to love him. She'd envisioned his child as her own.

Fool!

She had been bamboozled, and she ached from the fact that she had been too weak to prevent it.

If only she could avoid him forever.

Chapter Twenty-one

Her tenacity drove her, and Athena threw back the covers, standing to her feet. Brushing her teeth, she delved into the overnight bag, and decided on the blue running shorts and a gray tank top. She laced up the sneakers, planning a cathartic run in the mid morning sun.

Following the road up the mountain, she left the beach. The sun beat down on her, testing her endurance, but she did not relent. Pounding her feet into the road, she allowed the firm earth to strengthen her resolve.

No, he would not see what he'd done to her heart. She would not give him power over her happiness. She'd beat him in his own game.

No longer a fourteen-year-old girl who needed her brother to protect her honor, she was a grown woman. And a grown woman could have casual sex as well as any man could. She would not equate sex and love.

The sex was good, it was phenomenal, but she didn't have any other man to compare him to. Was this the way it was with everyone?

Lying to herself, she whispered under her breath. "You had a fling with a good looking man. It was purely physical and meant nothing more."

She tried to convince herself she could shut him out of her heart. No feelings, no exhilaration, no devastation.

She would see him at the wedding tomorrow, would have to face him. At the thought, her stomach curled and her feet stopped.

Bending at the waist, she rested her hands on her knees. She breathed heavy while drops of perspiration formed on her skin, and clung to her lashes. Surprisingly, she could not catch her breath.

Looking up, she blinked. A young man was walking toward her.

"Hi, you must not be from these parts," he said, reaching into his backpack and retrieving a bottle of water. "No local would think of taking on the sun at this time of the day."

Gratefully accepting the water, she drank before talking.

"Thank you. And no, I'm not from these parts. However, I should've known better. I've spent most of my summers in Greece, and I'm aware of how unforgiving the sun can be at this time. I'm very lucky you were coming down the road just now."

"I wouldn't say lucky." The man glanced at the old agricultural road and a Vespa parked against a tree. "You're giving the road quite a beating. *Eh?*"

She laughed, welcoming the vision into her mind. If she were one of her brothers a few years ago, she would have loved to pick a fight just to pound her fists into someone.

"My name is Gianni."

She extended her hand and introduced herself. "Athena."

"Athena, I was on my way to the beach for a cool drink, and from the look of things, you could use one too. Why don't you join me?"

Tensing, she was ready to reject his invitation when he emphasized his intent of friendship.

"My fiancée will be joining me there in a while, and she's been looking for a partner to beat up the tourists with. I didn't make the cut." He made a look of defeat, shrugging his broad shoulders together and slumping his back.

She began to laugh, recognizing the comical, non-threatening tone in his voice. "Sure, thanks," she said and fell in step beside him.

When they got to the beach, she had a tall glass of fresh orange juice and a toast of cheese and ham. They talked about the weather, the anticipated busy tourist season, and mundane work details new friends discuss before his cellular rang. Gianni checked the number and immediately flipped it open.

"No, everything is fine." Gianni smiled, but diverted his eyes from her. "I understand… yes… absolutely. I will see you later."

"That was my fiancée, she can't make it. I'm sure you will meet her soon." He pushed back in his chair and flashed a familiar smile.

Where had she seen that smile before?

Standing, she extended her hand. "Well, then thank you for the rescue and the breakfast, but since my future sparring partner has been delayed, I need to get going. It was nice to meet you, Gianni."

He shook it with the affability of an old friend and assured her they would meet again.

She walked along the hot sand, carrying her running shoes in one hand. Moving close to the water, she relished the waves gently lapping against the shore, and occasionally, her feet.

Once back in the cabana, she found the phone Spiro had packed and called Heather.

"Hi, where are you?" her friend asked in concern.

"I'm at the beach, getting ready for a swim." Athena succeeded in composing her voice and covering her anguish. "I just need a little time to myself before leaving for Crete, so I'm staying on the beach for the day."

Athena refused to trouble her friend the day before her wedding. She would erect a wall around her heart and carry on as if nothing was wrong.

"Is Alexandros with you?"

"No. I want to rest and take a tan today." Athena sounded surprisingly convincing.

"You're crazy to pass up a minute with him. You two are great together."

Athena's heart wrenched as she listened to her best friend tell her how happy she was for her, what a great couple they made, and that pretty soon she could see them repeating the week's events. This time for Athena's wedding.

Athena steadied her breath and blinked back the tears Heather couldn't see. "Yeah, yeah. You're such a romantic. I have to go, the wind is picking up, and my towel and book are flying away. I'll see you in the morning. Love you."

She closed the phone before her friend could respond and fell into the plump pillows on the couch.

She could do this. It was only one day, and if Heather did not know she was hurting, no one would. Nothing was going to ruin her friend's wedding. She would ignore the pain in her heart, the ache in her body, and the tears in her soul. She'd put on her practiced boardroom face for the wedding, and run like mad afterwards.

Athena went swimming, her tears melting in the salty water. Exhausted, she swam to shore and lay on the towel she had stretched out on the black sand. Her thoughts started racing again and she quickly stood as if to walk away from them.

Picking up two magazines from the kiosk by the *taverna*, she tried every which way to concentrate on fashion. She loved Italian shoes. Yes, she was going to buy herself a pair of those cute sandals in each color. Blue was in this summer and she looked good in blue. The natural makeup look was in, and curls were finally making a comeback.

She leafed aimlessly through the magazines. Finally, she tossed them aside. She did not care what they said.

Watching the sun make his way to its resting place for the night, she realized she was lonely. Emptiness had settled deep inside her, a hollow feeling in her heart. Determined not to wallow in self-pity, she decided to go shower and return to the *taverna* for an early dinner. Then she'd get some sleep and be ready for tomorrow.

Rising to her feet, she could feel something electric in the air. The fine hair on the back of her neck stood at attention as she walked back to the cabana. Pushing her shoulder against the door, she found no resistance, and it swung open.

She gasped. Her gaze swiftly traveled over his face. Alexandros' eyes were immense, dark stubble laced his jaw, and his hair was disheveled. He was still striking to look at. Her heart squeezed in her chest.

He extended his arm capturing her behind the neck, and swiftly sealed his mouth over hers. Her heart skipped as he curled his fingers into her hair and held her against him.

He prompted her lips to part, filling the soft, hot void with the demanding need to possess her. Weakness spread through her body as he held her close to him, her breasts swelling against his chest. He placed his lips to her ear breathing fire through her.

"You will never do that to me again."

Everything began spinning and her legs released her. The room went dark.

She resurfaced and saw concerned confusion staring at her. Determined that Alexandros would not find any answers in her eyes, she shuttered them with her dark soft lashes.

You can do this. You feel nothing. You're strong and carefree. His touch is only physical, on the skin. Your heart is safe.

She tried to focus again. "Hello, Alexandros."

"Are you okay, *agape mou*?"

"Yes, yes. Please move away, and give me some space." She worked hard to shield her eyes from emotion, but her hand trembled as she pushed at his thigh.

"Slowly, *paidi mou*, you may faint again." He shifted his body, giving her a few inches to sit up.

"I'm fine." She waved his hand away and tried to increase the distance between them. "I just had too much sun." She avoided his gaze. "I need to get up. Have some water…" to rinse the taste of him out of her soul. How could hate and love walk in tandem in her heart?

"I'll get you a drink." He stood and cleared his throat. "We need to talk. You must tell me what has upset you so much that you walked away from me. I don't understand any of it."

His words shocked her. The wall between them was back. She swung her legs over the bed he had carried her to and began walking toward the bath.

"No, we do not need to talk. I want to shower."

"Suddenly you don't welcome my touch, and you refuse to look at me. You fainted for no good reason."

"That's not true. I stayed in the sun too long. That's all. Don't make it a big deal. I simply need to shower."

"Why are you running from me again? You should listen, and you should talk to me, not wash me out of your life. Be reasonable."

She remembered her resolve. He wouldn't see how she really felt, he could not hurt her, and she would attend the wedding, escaping him immediately afterwards.

"Listen, darling." She'd never heard her voice sound like that before. "There is nothing wrong. I'm going to take a shower and then go out to eat. I'm hungry." She conjured a smile over her shoulder, tossing her head as she walked toward the bath.

She hoped he would grow tired and leave. Perhaps he would go for a walk to stretch his legs and she could leave instead. Wishful thinking.

"I'll be right here," he informed her of his intentions to stay and walked into the living room. Glancing back, she saw him sitting on the couch with his leg crossed over his knee.

Taking a deep breath, she walked into the bathroom and locked the door. Turning on the shower, she went back to the door to listen. Nothing.

Leaning her back on the smooth wooden surface, she inched down to the floor.

Chapter Twenty-two

Dressed and ready to go, Athena entered the living room. Alexandros looked up with brooding eyes and examined her from tip to toe. He stood, crossed over to her, and took her arm.

"Let's go." His voice was edged with annoyance, his hold a little too strong. He dragged her out of the cabana and to the car. It would be futile to argue with him, and frankly, she did not have the energy.

He deposited her in the passenger seat, walked around the car, and folded his long legs into the driver's side. They drove in silence along the cliffs, and suddenly he turned right taking them higher still.

"Where are we going?" she whispered.

"To eat. You are hungry, no?" His tone was abrupt, his eyes dark and narrow. "Don't tell me you've developed an aversion to Greek food as well."

He had no right to be angry with her. She was distraught because of him. When he'd stop the car, she would let him know exactly what she thought.

I cannot do this anymore. I don't know how to pretend that it doesn't matter. I'm beat and can't play.

He shifted gears and gently settled a large hand on her thigh. His fingers caressed her softly, but closed tight as he began to talk. "I spoke with my father this morning."

"He promised. He gave me his word." Her voice cracked. "He told you where I was?"

"No, Baba's a stubborn mule and refused to let me know. He insisted that I let you be."

"How did you find me?"

"I saw the driver by the port this afternoon. Concerned about you, Demosthenis asked if he could bring you anything to the cabana. He said you only had a small overnight bag."

"I see." She looked straight ahead as the car negotiated the sharp turns.

"No, *agape mou*, you don't."

She swallowed the lump in her throat and waited for him to continue.

"I realize that I made a big mistake, and I need you to forgive me."

Oh, *Thee mou*! Why was he doing this to her? He was toying with her heart, and she could not listen. "Please, don't say anymore. I can't do this. I just want the weekend to finish and to return to my life."

Guilt tugged at Alexandros' gut. He'd never imagined she would be so upset. He wanted to make her happy, not to smother

her spirit. At least now, she was listening to him. He had a chance to set it right.

His fingers relaxed, and he brought the car to a halt at a *taverna* sitting atop the cliff. Strings of light ran along the trellis, illuminating the little tavern on the dark cliff. The harbor was below them, and the lighted boats sparkled like jewels on the dark smooth sea.

Guiding her along the terrace to a candlelit table on the edge, he pulled out her chair and stood behind her, waiting for her to sit. His hands cupped her shoulders, and he bent to whisper.

"I'm sorry."

She quivered.

He sat snugly beside her, not wanting to let her go. He had never thought his actions would bring about these consequences. He'd been careless, selfish, and inconsiderate of her needs. He truly believed he could have fulfilled them all.

Keeping physical contact with her, lightly stroking the inside of her wrist, he ordered a bottle of *nikteri* and a plate of *mezedes*. Running the back of his fingers down her beautiful face, he placed his thumb on her lips, judging her readiness to hear him.

"*Agape mou.*"

Lifting her glass with shaky hands, she took a sip of wine, and then bit her bottom lip. He returned his thumb to her mouth, asking her to listen.

"I will not lose you. You can work for Luca as long as you please. It doesn't change how I feel about you."

"It's not about work, it's—"

"Shh, *agape mou.*" His thumb rested on her lips. Alexandros would do anything to make her happy. "Please listen to me. I've been doing a lot of thinking, and I was wrong to expect you to change your whole world. If you don't want to live in Greece, we can live in New York. I'll headquarter there. Costa will be here, and I'll fly in as often as is necessary. Say yes, Athena, say you will marry me. I want you to be mine—*panta,* forever."

"I can't." Her lips trembled.

"Why? Have you given your word to someone else?" He wiped a tear escaping her eye.

Thee mou, thankfully she has only given her word, her body she gave to me.

He felt the pang of guilt shred his gut again. This time he was really selfish. He wanted her all to himself.

"I will take care of it. We'll break the engagement, tactfully."

"No," she said, a small sound escaping her throat. "There is no one else for me."

"I want to take care of you, to make you my wife, to love you everyday of my life." He caught another tear and bent to place his lips on her wet cheek. "Do you love me?"

He swallowed the knot choking him. The truth would determine his next action.

"Yes, Alexandros, I love you. You're the only man I've ever loved. Last night you shattered my heart, and now it can not be pieced together."

Tears were coming too fast. Her eyes were red and swollen. He couldn't understand how their love could hurt her.

"We can go anywhere you want. You don't have to be involved with a Greek in Greece. I will go with you. *Agape mou*, I'll be happy and make you happy no matter where we choose to live. As long as we're together."

"Alexandros, if you really care for me, you'll agree with one request."

"What is in you heart? Tell me, and I'll make anything you want happen. You have my word. Anything to make you smile, to stop those tears from burning your beautiful eyes."

Her knees shook in a quick up and down motion. She barely looked at him; rather she stared at the knot she was twisting her hands into.

"I want a truce. I don't want to fight with you, it hurts too much."

Her blunt honesty hit him hard.

"I want to enjoy the wedding tomorrow. I don't want Costa and Heather to know anything is wrong. It's the most special day in their lives, nothing should ruin it." Her gaze met his, and there was pleading in her eyes.

"We'll enjoy the wedding, together."

"Okay, but no more talk about last night. No talk about us. I cannot do this. We will be civil and mature towards each other. If you still want to, we can talk after the wedding."

"Absolutely," he said, wondering if they were discussing the same things. What was she saying? Was she planning to walk out on him?

"My brother is scheduled to arrive in the morning, and I don't know what to do. I don't want to see him. And, I don't want him to see me like this. He can see right through me."

"Do you want to see him after we've settled this?"

"I have no choice. I will see him at the church. We'll deal with us after the wedding. Will you keep your distance and remember the truce?"

Pride was starting to intervene. She could not want more than he'd offered her. In his desire to make Athena his, he'd made a mistake, he hadn't committed a sin. She was not making any sense.

Regardless, he'd given her his word, and he would respect any request she made. He'd deal with Demo on her behalf. Hoping she would realize she wasn't being reasonable, he nodded his head in confused silence.

They finished their meal in forced politeness, settling the bill in a hurry. He drove to *Kalithea* and bid her goodnight at the main entrance with a simple kiss on the cheek. He walked to the study at the other end of the villa, as far away from her room as possible without leaving her completely alone.

Athena opened the door to her room and found herself standing in a garden. Apparently, Alexandros had flowers delivered for the previous night, and they filled the room with an exotic aroma that was rousing. The bittersweet emotion took control of her, and she lay on the bed, crying into a soft wet pillow.

Tears poured from her eyes in an endless stream. This had been the last night with the man she loved. He may be sorry, but she could never forgive his transgression.

She couldn't bear the thought of him seeking gratification with another woman. Even though she'd given herself to him completely, it had not satiated his physical passion. She didn't know how to pleasure him, not the way he was accustomed.

She'd taken what he had given her, had drowned in the tidal wave of pleasure he bestowed on her, but she was not enough for him. He had wanted more. He'd looked for and had found more.

Her body filled with pain. Before today, she would never have entertained the thought of forgiving a man for betraying her. She had to remain strong. She had to listen to her head and not her heart. How could she ever trust him again?

She heard the Ducati zoom away. Was Alexandros leaving the house in the middle of the night to find the green dress? Why had she not fought to keep him?

Pain engulfed her. She walked out to the side veranda and watched the motorcycle's headlight wind through the cliff side.

Alexandros needed to clear his head. None of this made sense. He drove around the island, pushing the Ducati's limits. Pulling up in front of a *kafeneion,* where only men gather, he walked up to the cousins who had finished the dance with him the night before, Spiro and Gianni.

They ordered a round of beers and began to talk.

"What happened to our smooth cousin? You've never introduced a woman to the family before."

"Spiro, I plan to make that woman my wife." Alexandros answered, a big weight lifted off his chest with the admission.

"It must be something in the air. Both of you, so fast." Spiro hit his cousin's back and laughed. "I hope it's not contagious."

"We should be so lucky," Gianni said, flipping his *komboloi*. "I spent some time with Athena, and she seems fantastic."

"She is. When did you see her?" Alexandros placed a hand over Gianni's *komboloi* and stopped it from moving.

"Your father asked me to keep an eye on her at the cabana. She wanted to stay alone, and he wasn't comfortable with that. I stayed in the cabana next door to hers, and we ran into each other in the morning."

"How could you lose your future bride and give her so much room away from you?" Spiro continued to tease his cousin. "Any one of us could have stolen her out of your arms."

"Cut it out, I'm not in the mood for you right now."

"Hey, I'm sorry. I meant no disrespect, Alexandros. I was only joking."

Alexandros nodded and accepted his apology.

"I'll be right back." Spiro stood. "I need to pick up some cigarettes."

Alexandros watched Spiro stroll to the kiosk on the corner, knowing he had not said anything out of malice. Spiro was ignorant of the events that had transpired since the family party and didn't understand the current situation.

"Gianni, tell me what happened in the morning and how she didn't recognize you from the party." He leaned back on his chair and pulled his own *komboloi* out of his pocket.

"Well, she met a lot of us at the party, and I only said hello there. When your father asked me to keep an eye on her, I washed the gel out of my hair and the curls returned. I put on my sunglasses and followed her on the Vespa as she went for a run around eleven o'clock today."

"A run at that time?"

"Yes, and let me tell you, I don't know what happened between you, but she was giving the road a pounding. She was very upset. And from the look of it cousin, if you want to make her your wife, you would do best not to cross her in the future. She is incredibly determined."

"When did you talk with her?"

"We went for a snack to Makis *taverna*."

Even though his father had arranged for Gianni to watch over her, Alexandros was growing jealous. She'd gone off with another man.

"I saw her suddenly stop running, and she started to look sick. I walked up, offered her some water, and we got to talking."

Gianni quickly clarified the event. "When I invited her to the *taverna* she hesitated, so I assured her my fiancée was meeting me. I made up a story about how they would enjoy each other's company and all."

"Thank you for looking after her."

"You'd do the same for me, for the woman I love. She's special, and you are lucky. I saw you come over in the afternoon, and I called your father to tell him I was leaving. Why are you here? Is she still at the cabana?"

"No, she's at *Kalithea*."

"I have to ask again. Why are you here?"

"I cannot be so close to her, and not be with her." Alexandros snapped the worry beads into his palm and let out an agitated breath. "Something happened and she is very annoyed. But it makes no sense."

"You'll figure it out. She's worth it. Go back to her and maybe she'll tell you. Some idiot probably told her something ridiculous. You know how jealous people can get."

"One more beer, and I'll be on my way."

Alexandros arrived at *Kalithea* in a calmer frame of mind. He would deal with this in the morning and the explanation would be right in front of him. He undressed and could not resist walking to Athena's room. Needing to check on her, and to know she was all right, he opened the door.

She was lying with her back to him. Her hair spread on the pillow and her breath soft and steady. He bent to kiss her, running a tender hand over the curve of her waist. Her slender hand covered his and held it against her. Alexandros did not wait for a formal invite. He lifted the sheet and gently got in beside her. Spooning her warm body, he curled his arm around her waist and pulled her closer to him.

Chapter Twenty-three

Athena awoke and felt Alexandros' warm breath against the nape of her neck. She didn't stir, not wanting to wake him. Closing her eyes, she lay still and drifted in and out of a sweet sleep. When Alexandros woke half an hour later, she remained motionless. Whispering something she didn't hear, he kissed her shoulder and got out of bed.

Moments later, he returned to speak through the window.

"You have about an hour before we leave. I assume you'll be helping Heather dress for the wedding."

"Yes, thank you. I'll be ready fast."

"Take your time. Costa will wait for her. I left you some coffee on the table… if you want it. I can't join you, but I'll be back by the time you're ready."

Only when she was sure he was gone, did she turn to face the window. She wanted to go to him, to ask him to hold her, and make the hurt go away. Her heart ached, and she craved his soothing touch. She had loved him. She still loved him, even after he'd betrayed her love.

Athena now understood the term *fool in love*. She was the fool. How could she still love him? Why did her heart ache, and why was he the only one who could fix it?

Showering, she let the tears run down her face and vanish into the clear water. The droplets urged her on, giving her the strength to face the day. She had a duty to fulfill, and she would bury her own needs to do it.

Slowly, she readied herself to face the family and friends she'd laughed with only days ago. Athena made a mental note to smile more as she applied makeup under her eyes to hide the puffy darkness. She pinned her hair high and allowed a few tendrils to fall. Stepping into her simple, but very elegant blue linen dress, she was satisfied with her appearance.

She gathered the makeup case and the hair styling tools into a bag and went to tell Alexandros she was ready. He was sitting at the table outside the kitchen. His eyes lit up as she approached.

"You look beautiful."

"Thank you. You're not dressed yet?"

"No, I'll dress after I return from the airport." He paused. "I saw Gianni at the *kafeneion* last night. He told me he spent a bit time with you yesterday on the beach."

"Yes, we had a light lunch. You know him?"

Relief spread through her. He had seen Gianni last night... at the *kafeneion*, a traditionally all male hangout. It explained why he smelled of alcohol and cigarettes when he came home. She had not talked to him, she hadn't told him she had lain awake waiting for him to return. She'd held his hand, inviting him into her bed, and thankfully, he'd stayed. Finally, she'd been able to sleep.

"Gianni is my cousin." Alexandros did not elaborate why Gianni was there or how he had come to talk to her.

"Oh, he is very nice." She waited quietly for him to get up, but instead he pulled out the chair beside him and asked her to sit. She sat.

"Athena, I spent the night trying to think what else might be bothering you. I cannot figure it out, *agape mou*. You need to help me with this, you must tell me."

"I don't want to discuss it." She stood to walk away, and he swiftly shackled her wrist.

"I want to discuss it. You're being totally unreasonable, and frankly, I don't enjoy drama like this."

"The problem is the things you do enjoy. That is the problem. And I will not have any of that in my life." She snapped her hand away. "Now you're even going back on your word. You agreed to a truce. You agreed that we'd enjoy the wedding in a dignified and mature manner."

"You mean a cold manner. Fine. If that is what you want, that is what we'll have. I won't beg you to explain. You want to be stubborn and act like the world has crashed about you, go right ahead. I will not tolerate it anymore. This is ridiculous!"

The small vein at his temple pulsed. He was angry, and she watched him speechless.

"No one can solve anything without knowing what it is, and I'm no exception."

"You have no right to speak to me like that. I'm not the one who plays games with relationships. I value the people around me, and I value the man in my bed."

"And I don't? I do not value *you?* What do I have to say to convince you of it? I told you I love you. I told you I wanted to marry you. I told you I would go to the other side of the earth for you. I can't think of anything else to say. I have nothing else to say. I'm done talking. You win. A cold civilized interaction at the wedding it is then." He grabbed the car keys and started for the drive. "Come on. There is much to do."

In silence, they drove to Villa *Cardia Mou.* She closed her eyes and tried to control her feelings, not wanting Heather to guess she was upset. When they reached the villa, she hastily opened the door and climbed out. Before closing it, she leaned in and met his gaze.

"It's not what you said, it's what you did. Something that would drive me crazy each time you were not with me. That is no way to live. You and I, both, deserve better." She turned and walked up the stairs into *Cardia Mou.*

"Woman, you're driving me mad! Perhaps you're right and this is wrong after all," he called. "Never in my life have I experienced something like this."

Never in his life had Alexandros loved a woman as he loved her.

Shifting the car into first gear, he spun the tires out of the drive. He drove fast and sharp, inviting danger with each turn. The small airport came into view, and Alexandros parked to wait for the plane. It landed, and Demo walked toward the terminal. The men greeted each other and headed to the car.

"I guess my sister has bridesmaid duties to do and couldn't come. Is she still at your house?"

"Sorry, I dropped her off earlier. She wanted to help Heather get ready." Alexandros tried to sound light, he was honoring Athena's request.

"You look horrible, my friend. Please don't tell me you guys had a stag party last night and Costa is going to look as bad as you do. You should never have a stag party the night before the wedding."

"No, no party. Costa surely looks better than I do. And by the way, thanks for the compliments." He drummed his fingers on the stick shift.

"What happened? No joke, you don't look very good."

"Athena happened, that is what. She is angry for reasons I do not know, and I can't get her to talk to me. I feel like shaking some sense into that warped brain of hers."

"Hey, you're speaking about someone I love."

"Someone I love, too." He slowed for the turn. "I swear, Demo, let the earth open and take me if I'm lying, I love her. She is making me crazy and is pushing all my limits. She refuses to talk, or to tell me what bothered her."

"I don't know what to say. She looked happy a few days ago. Very happy. Athena looked like she was in love for the first time in her life."

"She will be angry when she finds out we talked, but she said you could see right through her. So I am asking you—what could make her like this? She admits to loving me, but she doesn't want me near her." He spoke in rapid-fire Greek drawing lines of concentration on Demo's brow.

"Did you ask her straight on? She's forward about things."

"I asked her to marry me yesterday, and she said no. Then she admitted she loves me, and that the problem wasn't what I said. It was what I did."

"Alexandros, I can tell you that honesty and dignity mean a lot to her." Demo's thought lines grew deeper. "I don't know you well, but I don't think you'd be dishonest or disgraceful."

"She must have guessed I would ask her to marry me. I thought she didn't want to move to Greece and change her whole life. I offered to work out of New York and move with her—"

"No, that doesn't sound right. That's just a smoke screen to keep from getting to love. To keep from exposing her heart to hurt. If she said she loves you, she has no problem with Greece and that silly No Greek Romance rule of hers."

"Did anyone hurt her in the past to cause this?"

"Talk to her, and you'll work things out." Demo slapped the other man on the back. "Now trust me, and go get cleaned up. Use some eye drops or something like that, and then go stand beside your brother. I'd choke Tony if he showed up at my wedding looking like you do."

Demo refused the use of the car and reminded Alexandros he needed a shave before meeting up with the family.

How Alexandros arrived at his father's house to meet with Costa, he didn't know. He, like Athena, put on his boardroom face and entered the house. The difference was his family saw right through it. They were not co-workers or casual acquaintances.

Athena made her way upstairs and opened the door to the master bedroom. The gown lay magnificently on the bed, and Heather sat in front of her vanity beginning a light application of makeup. She smiled in the mirror at her best friend.

"Good morning."

"Good wedding morning to you." Athena hugged her friend's shoulders. "You are the most beautiful bride. I can't wait to see you in the dress."

"Well you won't have to wait long. Did you bring the large curling iron?"

Athena made a grand gesture of removing it from her bag.

"Good, plug it in and start curling the bun. Chop, chop," Heather said, smiling and snapping her fingers. "Do you think you came with me to spend your time making sweetie eyes at my groom's brother all day? Nope, you're here to do my hair."

The women laughed, but the pain in Athena's eyes reflected in the mirror. Heather turned.

"What's wrong?"

"Nothing. I'm very excited to do your hair, my lady." Athena tried to sound funny while avoiding her friend's gaze.

"Then why are your eyes puffy and dark?"

"That's an easy one. I spent too much time in the sun and under the water yesterday. I read two books, and I didn't sleep much because I had to finish the second story to see if the prince got the princess."

"And did he?"

"In your case, he did." Athena squeezed Heather's hand.

"How's your prince today?"

"He is a toad."

"So you're upset. You had an argument with Alexandros. Do you want to tell me about it?"

"No, not an argument. We'll deal with it later. I promise to tell you how it goes as soon as I know. Now let me get to work. Curling iron please." Athena held out her hand like a surgeon requesting a scalpel.

"Costa says he really loves you. I agree with him, and I think you love him too. He's a great guy, and he isn't bad to look at either."

"Mmm." Athena hesitated as she wrapped the first strand around the curling iron.

"I must say this, and then I'll stop. Don't, *do not*, cut off your nose to spite your face. Do not close down. Doing so is the only thing that'll hurt you."

"Okay, okay. But now we must give our attention to your hair."

Chapter Twenty-four

Tradition dictated the bride would walk through the town so that everyone could witness her journey to the church. Athena carried the bride's train as they strolled along the curvy streets and accepted the town's good wishes for a fertile, prosperous, and happy life. She pasted a smile on her face and nodded to the crowd.

The bright, cheerful interior of the church was full of family and friends. The traditional ceremony was an hour long, and Athena found it hard not to look at Alexandros. Placing the ornate wreaths on the couple's heads, Athena and Alexandros together crowned them King and Queen to each other in God's kingdom. They joined the newlyweds in their first steps as husband and wife, and stood beside each other as they sponsored brother and friend.

Athena exited the church on Alexandros' arm. She forced a smile on her face, while her heart ached from his touch. He was doing what she had asked, no one knew anything, and no one seemed to realize they were hurting.

The limousine pulled away and the guests began to walk towards the reception. Athena dropped Alexandros' arm and walked toward her brother. Demo hugged her, and she held him a second longer that usual.

Demo brought his lips to Athena's ear and whispered, "Talk with him, give it a chance." Then they continued to talk with the other guests.

Spiro stepped up to walk beside Alexandros. "Let her go. If it is meant to be, you will be together in the future."

"Baba, this doesn't make sense. I love her. I know she loves me. She completes me, and we need each other. Yet, she doesn't want to be with me. I cannot understand."

"Alexandros, it takes more than love to build a true relationship. Compassion, respect, faith and trust are paramount. You compromised her trust when you chose to sleep with another woman."

"What?" Alexandros stopped mid-stride. "Who told you such a lie?"

The older man looked at his son in dismay. "*Paidi mou*, I am sorry. I've misjudged the situation. For the first time in my life, I will break my word, my word to your Athena. I must end this, and you need to know."

"What are you saying, Baba?"

"The night of the party I found Athena crying in the garden. At first, she wouldn't tell me what had happened, and I feared the worst. She assured me she was physically fine, just upset. When I told her you would take her home, she became more distraught. She didn't want you. I could not understand."

"Baba, get to the point. What happened?"

"She saw you go into the bedroom with a woman to have sex."

"You believed that? You couldn't set her straight?"

"Athena heard you say you were waiting for the other woman all night. You locked the door for privacy. Alexandros, I had to offer her my help. It was the only decent thing to do. She was hurting, and I promised not to tell you."

Alexandros kissed his father heartedly on the cheek. "It's okay, you were looking over the woman I love." Relief entered his heart. "I can understand, and this finally makes sense. I have to go find her. I'll explain later."

He spotted Athena walking with Demo and quickly made his way through the crowd. Curling possessive fingers around her arm, he dragged her to the side. She tried to pull away, but he held her tight and refused to let her go.

Alexandros met Demo's gaze and silently expressed he had discovered the problem. Demo encouraged his sister with a pat on the arm and continued walking to the reception.

Alexandros couldn't wait and locked his lips to hers. She tried to resist, but he would not allow it.

He hugged her closer and spoke into her ear. "We need to clear things now, not later. I love you so much, and I can't stand to be without you for one more minute. We'll talk now."

The other guests passed and they stood alone in the street.

"I can't share you, it hurts too much." She turned to hide the tears behind her eyes.

"Athena, I'm yours, only yours. Look at me, and you will see that. It won't work if you don't trust me. *Agape mou*, look in your heart and tell me what you see."

Her beautiful eyes grew big, and she slowly said, "There is pain and love. Love for you."

"Yes, and my heart overflows with my love for you. Now answer me the most important question. Can that love overcome what has come between us?"

Athena's face was red with strain. She was hurting, but if she didn't trust him, nothing he could ever say would ever soothe her. Frustrated, he acknowledged she had to find it within her to trust him.

"I saw you with the woman in the green dress. You went into the bedroom, and you locked the door for privacy. But, I love you too much not to hear your explanation. Yes, I will trust what you have to say. Please tell me."

Unable to hide his relief, a smile spread across his face and he laughed loudly.

Tears began to stream down her cheeks.

"No, no don't cry. You didn't see correctly, *agape mou*—"

"Don't deny it." Athena interrupted him. "I saw you. You said you couldn't wait for her to get there."

"I don't deny that. Don't cry and just listen."

He was happy. He was elated. She trusted him to explain and she wanted to listen. He laid a full strong kiss on her open lips and crushed her to him.

"Now, don't let your imagination work anymore." He spoke quickly, reluctant to let her hurt a minute longer. "The green dress woman was Katerina, my personal assistant. I was waiting for her to deliver something to me. She couldn't come any earlier because it was her nephew's christening day. She arrived with the helicopter during the party. I planned to go to Athens myself, but I couldn't leave you. I wanted to spend every moment with you."

"Then why the secrecy? Why the locked door?" Her voice was steadier now.

"I didn't want you to see what she was bringing. I wanted to surprise you with it in the morning."

"You were not making love to the green dress woman?" Athena met his gaze, the horror fading from her eyes.

"No."

"I went through two days of hell", she breathed, shaking her head and massaging her temples. "I thought you had used me, and then I thought I wasn't enough for you."

"You are everything I've always wanted. You are all I need. *Agape mou*, I was in hell with you, we just could not see each other through the flames. I thought you didn't want me because of who and what I am. That rule of yours played like a broken record in my head. I didn't know where you were, I had to find you, and make you see I was the exception to the rule." He stood silently watching the expressions on her face, the face of the woman he loved.

"You are the exception," she breathed, bringing her lips to his.

"You make me the happiest man to walk this earth." A low groan emanated from deep in his throat.

He took her hand leading her toward *Kalithea*. She had to walk fast to keep up with him.

"We need to go to the reception. They'll miss us," she said, reaching the entrance.

"All I need is you." He pulled her into his arms and kissed her. Her lips parted, her breasts peaked against him, and he fit his slender hips against her, letting her feel his soaring hunger.

Warmth filled Athena, and she brought her lips to his, regretting she had doubted him. The heat in her body intensified, turning her insides to hot liquid. Her heart was pounding with the realization of his reciprocated love.

He situated her arms around his neck, and raised her body parallel to his, cupping her rounded buttocks as he carried her up the private, tree-lined path to *Kalithea*. Linking her legs around his waist, she buried her lips against his neck.

His fingers worked to unbutton her dress, exposing her back to the cool shaded air. Settling against him as he opened the bedroom door, she couldn't stop kissing the man she loved with all her heart.

Before he stepped through the doorway, he looked at her and pushed back a tendril of hair that swept across her cheek.

"I cannot wait until later. Patience has never been a virtue with me, and when I try to exercise it, I fail miserably." He lowered his head, brushed her lips, and said in a husky groan, "Athena, will you marry me?"

"Yes." Finding his mouth, she couldn't get enough of him.

He then walked into the room, and she slid down his body, her feet meeting the floor.

Alexandros' fingers released the thin straps of her dress, and it dropped to reveal her swollen breasts and more. He pursed his lips as first his eyes, then his hands, traveled from the curve of her neck, to the swells on her chest, to the curve of her hips, down her long legs, removing her panties in a swift move.

"*Thee mou*, all of this is mine," he drawled in Greek.

His mouth retraced the path, slowly, sensually taking her to the rim of a volcano about to explode, leaving a trail of fire on her skin. He kissed the center of her womanhood, caressing her inner core, sending her to a place where sheer pleasure reigned.

The moans leaving her lips called for him to catch her as she returned to the here and now. He did. Once steady, she led him to their bed, directing him towards the pillowed softness below and covering his body with her own above.

He groaned as she showed him how quickly she'd learned from him. She caressed his body with every inch of her own, and when he called to her, she brought her lips to his, letting her hair fall around his face as she guided him into her. Gently, he filled her, and they rode together to ecstasy.

She laid her head on his chest and snugly nestled her torso against him. He wrapped his leg over her, and she reveled in the moment of knowing that they belonged to each other.

"Never doubt how much I love you, my Athena. I knew I wanted to make you mine from the first moment I saw you."

"Yiayia told me the Strintzaris men have no timeline. I agree with her. I love you."

"*Agape mou*, you've lost me." He looked confused.

Athena laughed. "It's woman talk. Something we do amongst ourselves."

"I'll take your word for it. I need you to do something."

"Now?" she asked, wetting her lips with the expectancy of his request.

"Now." A seductive smile spread across his handsome face. "Get out of bed, please."

This was not the request she was expecting. Her mouth opened and he immediately lavished it with a long sensuous kiss. "Now, please, stand up, and turn your back to me." His intriguing voice held a promise, compelling her not to question his motive.

Her feet touched the cool marble floor, and she took a few steps away from the bed. The sea breeze brushed across her heated body sending goose pumps to her bare flesh.

Alexandros brought his body against her back instantly warming her. He wrapped the sheet around them and smoothed the bumps away.

"I want to see your face in the sunlight." He steered her onto the terrace.

She could feel his heart beat in tandem with hers, his breath heavy.

"When it comes to you, I cannot wait. I cannot be smooth and collected. I just want you for myself, and I want the world to know you are mine."

"I am, and I want the world to know you are mine too." She turned in his tight embrace as he shifted under the sheet.

"I can't wait for the priest to bless this." From behind her back, he revealed a box and opened it. The ring reflected the sunlight around them. "Allow me the honor of placing this token of my endless love on your beautiful hand."

She stared as he fit the ring on her wedding finger, and then raised it to his lips. "Thank you for making me the happiest man, *yineka mou*."

She whispered. "When did you get it?"

"I picked it out when we were in Athens. They needed more time for the setting."

"You're rather sure of me then."

"No, that's not it. I'm very insistent, and I would have kept asking you until you said yes."

"So when did you get the ring?"

"The night of the party. Katerina brought it."

She was speechless. How could she have ever doubted him? She sought his kiss, and trembled as she felt his love encompass her soul, completing the love she had for him inside her.

"I'm sorry." Tears threatened to flood from her eyes. "I'm sorry I doubted you, *andra mou*."

"No tears, unless they are tears of joy."

"They are." She held her hand up to the light and smiled at him. "Did I tell you, I love you?"

"I can't hear it enough. Why don't you do that now?" He took the words from her mouth and they made slow, tender love once again.

Alexandros and Athena arrived at the reception freshly showered and beaming blissfully just before sunset. The single women were gathering to catch the bouquet as Alexandros pulled her towards his parents.

"The bouquet. I have to get in line." She said tugging his arm in the opposite direction.

"Absolutely not. You're mine and definitely not available." He laughed and hugged her to him. He walked towards his parents squeezing her linked fingers in his.

As they approached Spiro, he smiled. "Is everything all right, *paidia mou*?"

Alexandros raised Athena's hand to show them the ring on her finger. "More than that, Baba. Athena has made me happier than I thought was possible. She has agreed to be my wife, the light in my life forever."

"Don't let the band leave before we book them again." Spiro winked at his wife, and his big arms engulfed Athena. "*Kori mou*, just tell me when."

Anna let a joyful tear slip, and looked at her oldest son with his Athena. She cupped the young woman's face with her palms and kissed her. "*Kori mou*, I knew I would meet your mother sooner, rather than later."

Athena looked for her brother. She met his gaze from the other side of the room. Demo motioned thumbs up as she waved her fingers at him showing him her ring.

Yiayia walked up to them, took Athena's hand and asked Alexandros, "When will this young woman officially become my granddaughter?"

"We haven't set a date, Yiayia. But if Athena agrees, as soon as my future in-laws can come to Greece would be nice. How about July, *agape mou*?"

Athena winked knowingly at Yiayia. "I think that's agreeable, and just right."

About the Author

Born in Athens, Greece, and raised in the States, Aleka Nakis has straddled the Atlantic and has had one foot on each continent for many years. Aleka loves to travel and does so with every excuse available to her. Blending her life passions of story telling, travel, and exotic cultures, Aleka transports her readers to the magical world of romance.

http://www.alekanakis.com

Book Two of The Greek Series:

The Summer Deal

by Aleka Nakis.

Samantha Mallone is a smart, beautiful redhead who is oblivious of the magnetic affect she has on her charismatic boss... International billionaires don't lie to get a woman, but Demosthenis Lakis does just that to lure his assistant to Greece. Unaware of her employer's true motivations, Samantha eagerly prepares for a summer in the Mediterranean when her psychotic-ex calls and threatens her, prompting Mr. Lakis to arrange for her to leave New York immediately. Abroad, Mr. Lakis changes the ground rules: They're in Greece where formalities are foreign. Samantha becomes Sammy, and Mr. Lakis becomes Demo. Sexual tension burns as the big-eyed Sammy tours the ancient ruins on Demo's arm and discovers his intent to show her there is more to their relationship than business. Proving to be unlike other men from Sammy's past, Demo puts their passionate summer deal to the test of a lifetime.

Read on for a preview.

The Summer Deal

By Aleka Nakis

Chapter One

Aggravated with the results of the day's interviews, Demosthenis Lakis didn't bother to look up when his office door opened and the last applicant approached his desk, her heels clicking upon his hard wood floor in a confident rhythm.

Instead, he took a deep breath and focused on the information in his hands. Miss Samantha Mallone's resume indicated that she possessed none of the qualifications he was looking for and required in an assistant.

"Hello. Thank you for meeting with me, Mr. Lakis."

The melodic voice seized his attention. His head snapped up and he shut the manila folder. "Ms. Mallone?"

The woman standing in front of him was a pure knockout. A bit short, but ooh, very shapely. Shiny red hair flowed over a cream-colored suit, forming an image of how it would look draped over his pillows.

As he pushed back his chair, the file slipped from his hand,

and paper littered his desk. Fumbling through the sheets, he gathered them into a pile, flipped the cover, and stood to greet his applicant.

"Pleased to meet you," he said, holding out his arm.

"Thank you, sir."

Her soft hand slid into his and he found it difficult to concentrate. A sweet citrus smell filled the air, and he was consumed with the urge to pull her against him and feel every inch of her.

Mustering all his strength, he jerked his hand back and smiled in a forced professional manner. *Obviously, it's a set up. It has to be. Why else would a gorgeous woman with no experience be here?*

His brother, and business partner, had to be behind this. Demo laughed and shook his head. This was just the sort of thing Tony would do. He'd dangle a piece of eye candy, useless for work, just to remind him that there was more to life than the office. His brother was always on his case about taking things so seriously. But someone had to, and Demo was not one to leave things to chance.

Taking a deep breath, he asked, "So how's Tony?"

"Excuse me? Who's Tony?" she replied, her emerald eyes growing confused under his examination.

Her hand fluttered to her throat and her fingers closed about a thin gold chain she wore around her beautifully sculpted neck. A bewildered look crossed her face, and her nose crinkled in concentration.

Damn! She wasn't a joke. His brother wasn't playing his typical games. She was real. A real applicant he'd have to professionally turn away, despite her personal appeal.

He might as well make this quick.

"I'm sorry, Ms. Mallone." Extending his arm, he indicated a seat, and then gulping a humble breath of air, he continued, "I thought you were a friend of my brother's. Shall we begin?"

She sat, crossed her legs, and folded her hands over her knee like a goddess. Smiling, she glanced around the room and let out a tiny sigh.

"Tell me a little about yourself."

Samantha cleared her throat and played with the chain around her neck. "I'd like to thank you for this opportunity, Mr. Lakis. I know it may appear that I lack formal training, but I can assure you, I'm more than capable of meeting your needs."

Demo had no qualms about that. He could think of many ways she'd meet his needs. And for everything else, he'd outsource the documents and hire a second receptionist for the filing.

"I'm in my final year of law school. I am a quick learner and very dedicated to my work..."

Watching her lips move, but not truly hearing a word, he lost himself in the song of her voice. Going against his initial plan of letting her out of their interview quickly, he did everything to prolong their discussion. He asked her about her university courses, limited work experience, and future aspirations in the legal field.

Her foot bobbed in a nervous motion that he found

hypnotic. *Cute ankles*. He could envision her toes curling on his lap. Where they painted red, or did they match the pale shade on her fingernails?

Damn! He was thinking about nail polish.

Real professional, Demo. A deal maker for sure.

"I could supply recommendations from professors I've worked with," she offered.

"No." He shook his head. "Your supervisor at Gyro King has written great things about you, Ms. Mallone, including that you were head cashier and helped with the paperwork. From your resume, I see you're familiar with a variety of word processing systems, including the one we use."

Standing to pace the room, he paused and stared out the twenty-fifth story window, down at the lights illuminating the paths in Central Park. A moment to collect his thoughts—that's what he needed. He didn't have time to play games. If she wasn't in direct sight, perhaps he could think logically, rationally—as a successful businessman should.

"I used the same system when I worked for the assistant dean as a student employee. Actually, I'm proficient in all of the popular word processing and business spreadsheet systems. I must admit: I'm a computer geek."

Demo turned in time to see a smile cross her lips as the room filled with a warm glow.

The woman was a computer geek? He couldn't suppress a chuckle. She looked like a nymph, or better yet a pixie, that could intoxicate a man. All he wanted to do was tangle his fingers in her coppery hair, bury his face against her creamy neck, and do things to her that would guarantee a sexual harassment lawsuit.

"I am proficient in all of the systems on the market."

"Very good." He captured her gaze. "However, the requirements for the position are extremely difficult and demand a great deal of initiative and excellent self-motivation."

Returning to sit behind his desk, he propped his elbows on either side of her resume. "The assistant who has been working with me for years has had unexpected personal issues and is not available to help train for any period of time. I will personally oversee her replacement for approximately twenty days, and then will leave for an overseas trip."

"Mr. Lakis, I'm a quick learner. You will not be disappointed in my performance if you decide to give me a chance."

Disappointment would not be an issue. But hiring Samantha Mallone was crazy. A former restaurant worker and computer geek was to assist him in running an international firm? He'd have to work twice as hard once she began.

"When are you available to start, Ms. Mallone?"

"Tomorrow, if you'd like."

What was wrong with him? He was turning into those men he despised: men who abused their power to seduce beautiful women into their beds. But he couldn't seem to help himself. He couldn't stop grinning.

Shrugging, he offered his hand. "Monday morning at nine will be fine. Welcome to Lakis International, Samantha."

"Thank you, sir."

She extended her hand, and he accepted it with great pleasure. His gaze settled on her full lips and he stared, mesmerized by their temptation.

"This is exactly the job I want. I won't make you regret it..."

Her full pink mouth moved, but once again, he heard no words. He wondered if she tasted as sweet as she looked.

"I can't wait to tell my fiancé," Samantha finished.

Lightning struck, freezing the grin on his face, and causing him to regret the first business decision made with his hormones. What had she said? Was it something about a fiancé?

Krima! This sunshine belonged to another man.

Running his fingers through his hair, Demo decided to think before he responded. He bit his lip and attempted an empathetic smile.

Professional. Be professional. This is not a personal relationship.

"That is good to know, Ms. Mallone. We have found when members of our team enjoy their job, and the circumstances fit their personal preferences, it is indeed an added bonus to their employment. I believe you will find the position challenging, but gratifying."

She nodded and eagerly added, "I'm sure it will be the perfect job. Thank you for the opportunity, sir. The hands-on experience before taking the bar exam will be great. And as I mentioned earlier, I am familiar with international law and it is a course of study I excel in."

"Fantastic. The packet the personnel director gave you during the first interview outlines the position's requirements. Please review it, and feel free to ask me any questions before you begin." He handed her his card. "Both the office and my personal phone numbers are there. You can reach me at any time on the second number."

She smiled and placed the card into a neat, leather dossier. "I'll be sure to complete the necessary documentation and leave it with the personnel department." She smiled and collected her things. "Thank you very much. I'll see you Monday morning."

Performing on autopilot, he walked his new employee to the door. Telling the receptionist to shut down the office and call it a night, he watched Samantha's curvy bottom step into the elevator.

"Samantha?"

"Yes, Mr. Lakis?"

"If needed, will you remain past the expected ten month term?" He hesitated, but added, "Until my assistant is ready to return to work?"

"Absolutely, sir." She smiled and raised her hand.

He nodded, and the elevator door closed.

Sighing, he stormed back into his office, shut the door, sat at his desk, and dropped his head into his hands. "What got into you?"

Demo had never made such a decision in his life. He hadn't built a multi-billion dollar firm on impulse or bad judgment. He had no idea what had possessed him with the cute redhead or why he'd let his hormones rule his brain. This was out of character for him. Perhaps a simple diversion would rectify the situation?

He leaned back from his desk and opened the top left drawer. Glancing through his personal agenda, he picked up the phone and dialed.

"Katrina, how are you? ...Yes, I know it's been a while. Work has kept me busier than I care to admit... But I have some time for myself tonight, and I want to ask if you will join me for dinner?"

Tapping his fingers on his desk, he swiveled his chair and patiently listened as his date explained how hard it would be to rearrange her schedule, but she would do it for him.

"Great. I'll be by at eight."

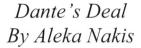

Dante's Deal
By Aleka Nakis

Two months before her twenty-third birthday, Sapphyra Morelli pumps herself up with confidence and corporate bravado and storms into her husband's conference room a changed woman. In spite of all her preparations, pride blinds her to the truth about the relationship she shares with Dante Morelli, and she cannot recognize that the life she craves is already her own.

Dante headquarters his business in the shady alleys of Naples, lives in the picturesque seaside of Positano, and keeps his wife on the busy avenues of New York City. Sapphyra is the young wife who he has been responsible for and whom he's held at arm's length, waiting for her to mature into a woman who knows her own mind and heart. As obligated by the contract, Dante accepts her in the boardroom as an equal.

Battling between the carnal need for his wife and the promise he'd made to her dying father to take care of her like he would his own sister, he decides he's entitled to Sapphy—at least for the two months remaining in their marriage contract. Because of his insistence that Sapphy stand beside him as his wife, the plan to be a real business partner expands to winning her husband's heart and body.

Visit Aleka @

www.AlekaNakis.com

https://www.facebook.com/alekanakis

Printed in Great Britain
by Amazon